THE HEIRLOOM

SECRETS OF SILVER GROVE

BOOK ONE

BLY FORSYTHE

To Chris, with all my love —

ONE

I rushed a brush through my long, brown hair, and threw on the clothes lounging on my laundry chair. My daily attire was a uniform of casual elegance; a simple sweater, jeans, and well-worn loafers were my armor against prying eyes.

I trudged into the kitchenette and grabbed my favorite, ironic mug; a thrifted cauldron that had seen more brews than I could count. I rubbed my eyes, dispelling any lingering sleep, and scanned the messy countertop that was strewn with unfulfilled Etsy orders, and simple potion ingredients.

I beckoned the bag of coffee grounds towards myself with a muttered spell and a casual flick of my hand, their earthy aroma filling the air as they floated into the mug. With another well-practiced incantation, I poured water into the mug, swirling my pointer finger clockwise and chanting a simple charm of warmth. As it heated to the perfect temperature, and the rich, aromatic liquid percolated, I leaned against the kitchenette, savoring the morning's tranquility.

A knock at the door startled me out of my reverie. I set my drink down and spelled my potion ingredients into a nearby junk drawer with haste before turning to the door.

"Iris!" A young woman's voice rang out, loud even against the barrier of the door.

I smiled softly and shook my head, my pounding heart settling at the familiar sound of my best friend's voice.

I disenchanted the lock, and the thunk of the dead-bolt was enough of an invitation that Thalia pushed the door open, her warm and knowing yellow eyes meeting mine. She had an uncanny ability to sense when something was amiss, even when I tried to keep my secrets hidden.

"Good morning, my elusive enchantress," Thalia greeted me with a grin. "I knew something was brewing in here. What magical mischief are you up to today?"

Thalia gracefully embraced the essence of gothic allure, adorned in a striking ensemble that seamlessly blended darkness with elegance. Her reddish-orange hair wrapped around her pale face, which framed mysterious yellow eyes. Against the porcelain canvas of her skin, a deep plum lipstick drew attention to her sharp, white teeth.

I chuckled. "Just a regular morning brew. But who knows what the day has in store for us?"

She winked at me, her eyes twinkling even in the dim light of the kitchen.

"You look stressed." She gave me a once-over and clucked her tongue. "Have you started having those nightmares again?"

I stared into my coffee mug, not wishing to meet her gaze. But the Werecat was astute, and my limited repertoire of spells could only do so much to hide the dark circles that my bad dreams had crafted.

Maybe if my training had been completed. Maybe if–I didn't allow myself to finish the thought. I forced my heartbeat to steady and met Thalia's unwavering gaze, shaking my head.

"Just all these orders I have to complete by the weekend. Everyone and their mom just has to have one of my custom centerpieces suddenly." I rubbed my temple in a show of stress. "But I shouldn't complain. Business has been great lately," I shrugged at my friend.

Thalia's piercing eyes bore into me, her suspicion clear. The vivid images of my nightmares lingered in my mind as I tried to conceal the weariness that clung to me. I silently urged my heart to maintain a steady rhythm; she didn't need to concern herself with my sleepless nights.

The fragments of my past, elusive and haunting, were resistant to the soothing touch of magic or the warmth of friendship. I reassured myself that they held no significance, just echoes of bygone moments. With practiced composure, I offered Thalia a small, reassuring smile, hoping to deflect any worries that might form from her feline instincts.

"If you say so," she said and blew the stray hairs from her face. "Grab your orders and let's get to the café. If I don't get a scone in my mouth immediately, then I might actually die."

I rolled my eyes at my dramatic best friend, but I still swept my orders from the island into a nearby tote bag, and slipped on my shoes. I motioned to Thalia, and she confidently strode to the door, as I followed closely behind.

The hallway stretched ahead, lined with doors decorated with personalized touches; each telling a story of its inhabitant. As we walked, the muted hum of conversation from neighboring apartments underscored the sense of community we were leaving behind, if only temporarily. I noticed the door across the hall had boxes next to it; someone was moving out or moving in.

The exterior of my apartment complex was coated

in a palette of muted pastel colors, complemented by well-tended gardens and climbing vines that gracefully climbed the walls, softening the edges of the structures. The windows, adorned with delicate curtains, hinted at the warmth within each unit. Flower boxes, carefully tended by residents, added splashes of color to the exteriors, creating a picturesque scene that felt right out of a storybook. My modest savings account I inherited when I was fourteen was to be thanked for my creature comforts.

We ambled along, and I appreciated the vibrant hues of autumn - deep reds, burnt oranges, and rich yellows painting the landscape. The air carried the scent of fallen leaves, their vibrant colors now a carpet beneath my feet.

The sunlight filtered through the branches of the trees, casting a cozy glow on the surroundings. I hugged my arms around my waist, feeling the chilly air nip at my cheeks, and walked in tandem with Thalia to the local café.

"- but who knows, maybe I'll even find my fated there." Thalia looked at me and tugged at the crescent-shaped jewel on her necklace.

"Uh..." I lifted a hand up and ruffled my long brown hair. "Find your fated where?"

The Werecat bared her longer than average eye-teeth at me and hissed with annoyance, before rolling her eyes impishly. I turned my full attention to her and nodded at her to continue.

"I *said* there's a ball coming up next month. My dad is closer to retirement, and is almost ready to leave the Clan to Ewan to take over, and have me assist and maybe lead another Clan. But those misogynistic by-laws say I have to be mated before I can lead, and If I don't find my fated soon, I'm worried that I'll be paired with *anyone* that can help the Clan's bloodline. Iris, I would just die if I was forever tied to some random asshole when my fated is out there," Thalia huffed. "But who knows, maybe I'll find my true fated at the ball and my father's worries will all be moot."

We reached the coffee shop, and I pulled the frosted glass door towards me. "Goddess help the poor sap chained to you, fated or not," I smiled as we walked into the cozy shop.

'Divine Bliss Espresso' was a place where time seemed to stand still, where the aroma of fresh brew and the soft murmur of conversation created a comforting cocoon. It was here that my façade as an ordinary suburban woman thrived. I grabbed our favorite settee closest to the large window near the front while Thalia ordered some midmorning teas.

Dumping my tote on the coffee table in front of me, I watched as my unfinished orders tumbled out. Twine, various small crystals, artificial greenery, and flowers looked back at me, ready to be molded into the witchy centerpieces of my customers' dreams.

I always laughed a little when fulfilling the orders; no one knew that a real Witch was behind the scenes, crafting their home decor. My online shop was adorned with enchanting photos and spellbinding descriptions. It portrayed an image of just another artisanal business.

If I can even call myself a proper witch, I moped.

I took a deep breath, attempting to dispel the last traces of the unsettling emotions that lingered within. Still, the echoes of the nightmare persisted, like whispers in the corners of my mind. I shook my head as if physically dispelling the lingering discomfort. Today was a new day, and I was determined to leave the haunting visions of the night behind.

Sauntering towards our spot with our drinks in her hands, Thalia drew the eyes of both male and female patrons. Her confident stride and athletic body came from years of training and working as a huntress for her Clan, and her presence exuded a captivating blend of strength and grace.

Mortals could always sense something different about us, especially Thalia. It wasn't just her physical prowess or her eyes that hinted at a more vertical pupil—there was an air of ancient knowledge, a wisdom earned through encounters with creatures of the wild and the unforgiving landscapes she traversed.

Few mortals were ever confident enough to woo the feline - humans were almost always more intimidated than intrigued. Mortals could never quite place the unease caused by being near an Occult, but their subconscious knew to stay away from the supernatural. I took my mug of lavender honey tea from Thalia's outstretched hand and inhaled the calming aroma that wafted from the steaming brew.

Two

I put the finishing touches on the third centerpiece and rotated my aching wrists. The delicate balance of floral arrangements and intricate details had finally converged into a stunning display I was proud of. A burst of Bouvardia blooms in subtle white hues rose from a rounded glass vase, creating a focal point that would captivate the eye.

Tapered candles in shades of plum were elegantly held by ornate gold holders shaped like ravens, and placed sporadically throughout the flowers. I finished the centerpiece by dangling a few malachite gems I wrapped in thin gold wire. As I leaned back to admire my work, the natural light played off the carefully chosen colors, casting a photo-worthy glow.

I looked over at Thalia lying horizontally on the café couch, her black combat boots dangling over the armrest lazily, a hand idly tugging the gem on her necklace back and forth, and a half-eaten croissant forgotten beside her while she played on her phone.

I turned back to my finished work and snapped a few pictures to update my clients on their new décor. Delicately bubble-wrapping them and placing the products in their boxes, I taped them firmly shut and stuck their labels on the top.

"Ready?" Thalia eyed my finishing touches and stood slowly.

"Yeah. I'm not working any more today. I always get so stiff when I'm doing repetitive tasks for too long," I confessed, rolling my shoulders to ease the tension.

As we gathered the carefully packed centerpieces, I couldn't help but glance at Thalia's phone. "What's got you hooked?" I asked with an eyebrow raise.

She smirked, her fingers tapping away on the screen. "Just some Werecat from the Lightpaw Clan that I've been messing around with. He wants to be my date to the ball, but I told him I'm already spoken for," she said and winked at me.

My eyebrow lifted. "And who is this mystery date you speak of?" The packages balanced precariously in my tote, the weight causing a slight strain on my shoulder. I ambled to the door, careful not to jostle the carefully crafted centerpieces within their boxes.

"You, obviously! I know it's hosted by my Clan, but *anyone* can find their fated at the ball, you know. All kinds of Occults will be there, Iris."

"Your dad finally opened up the guest list?" I asked her, not paying attention as I pulled open the door and stepped through. My face connected with a chest in a bespoke gray suit, and while I stepped back in surprise, I heard a cough from the gentleman. Rubbing my nose with my free hand, I looked up to see a pair of displeased brown eyes peering down at me.

"Smooth entrance," he remarked coldly.

The man was gorgeous. His chiseled jaw clenched in frustration at my mistake, his pale skin pink with irritation, and I took a step back. He was tall and slender, but I could see the muscles in his chest and arms pressing against his fitted button down. His russet eyes stared at me in annoyance.

"Next time, be more careful," he grumbled, his tone unyielding.

"It was a mistake. You don't need to get all worked up about it," I muttered under my breath, more to myself than to the retreating figure of the man in the suit. He stopped and glared at me for a moment, pressing his brows together in annoyance, before turning back towards the line in the café. I rolled my eyes and situated my bag before bracing the wind outside.

"What a prick, am I right?" I grumbled to Thalia. The nearest postal box was only about a block away, but I kicked myself for not bringing another layer to fight off the afternoon chill. She looked at me quizzically, putting her phone away.

"You know who that was, right? Adrian Grayson."

"The playboy that's supposed to take over his dad's tech company here in Silver Grove? Not impressed." I rolled my eyes.

Thalia shrugged. "I wouldn't mind finding out for myself if the rumors are true," she giggled. "They say he's an absolute animal in bed, and I wouldn't mind being the judge of that." She purred, her yellowish eyes dancing with mischief.

"Handsome or not, I don't know how anyone can stomach his complete lack of manners. If I acted like he did, I'd be a virgin until the day I died."

Thalia gave a hearty laugh, her head tilted and her mouth curled with mirth. "I'll always appreciate your unrelenting honesty."

"Wait, don't you do work for that company? 'Vulture Network Services'. That definitely rings a bell," I said.

"Our Clan takes on a lot of security gigs around Silver Grove, but my dad recently worked out a non-compete with Mr. Grayson. When I'm not helping my parents with Clan stuff, I'm doing front desk security at Vulture," Thalia shrugged. "I see Adrian around the building sometimes, usually with a different woman hanging onto his every word. But I guess at least he's at the office."

"When's your next shift?" I asked. "Want to do lunch on your break?"

"Thursday," Thalia replied. "Ewan is working too," she raised her eyebrow at me.

I ignored her and kept walking, not sure what to say about her older brother.

Why have I always felt so flustered around him? Maybe it was his confidence, his striking looks, or the way he effortlessly commanded attention. Whatever it was, it left me struggling to find the right words whenever he was around.

"Caught in the web of his charm again, huh?" she teased.

I laughed nervously, attempting to downplay the situation. "Oh, please. I was just... lost in thought."

"I know you've always been down bad for him, enchantress. But, whatever," Thalia smiled and graciously changed the subject. "What are your plans for the rest of the day? I have training across town with some new warriors in an hour. Want to come?"

I rolled my eyes, but there was truth in her words. No matter how hard I tried, Ewan had a way of leaving me speechless. I couldn't deny the attrac-

tion, but I also couldn't ignore the complicated feelings it gave me. We walked up to the post bin, and
Thalia lifted the handle so I could slip the mail
inside.

"I'm always game," I smiled.

———

We approached the gated community. The imposing
iron bars marked the threshold between Silver Grove
and the concealed quarters of the FrostFelt Werecat
Clan. To the oblivious eyes of mortals, it appeared as
an upscale neighborhood, its walls adorned with ivy
and lined with meticulously manicured lawns.

But the truth lay in the truth below the surface—
an invisible barrier that concealed the mystical happen-
ings within. My parents had been close with the Clan,
and their magic had helped create this sanctuary.
Thalia typed in the code and the gate opened, revealing
an expanse of Tudor-style homes.

The manicured lawn, a canvas of vibrant green,
stretched luxuriously at the front of the neighborhood.
A gentle breeze carried the scent of the freshly cut
grass, and I breathed in deeply. At the center of the
field, a group of athletic male and female Occults in
sleek workout attire engaged in a sophisticated pre-
training routine. Their toned bodies moved fluidly

through a series of exercises, and Thalia quickly changed into her tennis shoes.

"Don't wait up!" The Werecat called out to me as she jogged over to her fellow Clan members.

I grabbed a seat on a nearby bench and watched them get to work. Quick, agile movements defined the early exchanges as the Werecats circled each other, assessing distance and studying their opponent's tendencies. The occasional feint or quick jab served as a strategic probing, testing the waters and gauging reactions.

Tense muscles and focused expressions revealed the determination of the Clan members, while strategic smiles or nods showed a mutual respect for each other's skills. The ebb and flow of their training created a dynamic visual spectacle, a ballet of controlled aggression and tactical finesse. A petite blonde jogged up to me, her sleek ponytail bouncing in tandem with her steps.

"Hey, Iris!" she smiled at me warmly. "Want to join?"

I smiled back at her, then grimaced. "Hey, Lyra. I'll join when I'm feeling masochistic again. I think last time proved that a Witch trying to keep up with a Werecat is an exercise in futility."

Lyra laughed. "Well, the offer still stands! You know you're a part of the Clan. Especially for what your parents did for us–" She noticed my sour expression and tried to backpedal. "Oh! I mean–You–" She kept tripping over her words and I finally took pity on her.

"It's okay, Lyra. Let's catch up soon, okay?" I politely dismissed her.

She smiled again. "That sounds great! Bye, Iris."

I watched her jog back to the group, and I tried to focus on the Clan's training. Thalia ordered a two-mile run and came over to sit by me.

"Everything okay?" she asked. "Lyra looked pretty embarrassed when she re-joined us."

I nodded and put my head on her sweaty shoulder. "We took a trip down memory lane and I wasn't ready."

My best friend nodded and stroked my hair, keeping quiet. I was grateful to Thalia. She always seemed to know exactly what I needed. And right now, it was a long and comfortable silence.

THREE

Thalia excused herself to take a phone call, and I couldn't help but notice the subtle lines of agitation etched on her face. Her brow furrowed, and a flicker of concern danced in her eyes. Even from my spot on the bench I could see the tension in her body. She tugged anxiously at the moonstone pendant of her necklace, the colors dancing in the sunlight.

She approached me with a heavy sigh. "There's a land dispute with the Neighboring Werecat Clan," she confessed, her voice carrying the burden of responsibility. "They've reached out for our help, and I can't turn them away."

She looked at her phone again. "I'll have to rearrange everyone's work schedule to ensure we have enough warriors to assist them. It's going to be a logistical challenge, and not everyone will be thrilled about the sudden changes."

Her phone buzzed again and she huffed. "I need to head to the Clan house and get on my computer. Text you later, witchy woman." She wiggled her fingers in farewell and walked off, her phone pressed to her ear.

———

The brisk wind tousled my hair as I began the long walk home.

I'm taking the bike next time, I grumbled to myself.

As I approached my apartment building, I couldn't shake the weariness that clung to my bones. The prospect of some quiet solitude, my refuge within these walls, felt like a healing balm to my restless soul. Thalia's voice lingered in my mind as she assured me she would reach out later.

Unlocking the door to my apartment, I stepped into the cozy abode I had carefully crafted over the years. The soft glow of ambient lights and the familiar scent of lavender welcomed me home. I kicked off my shoes and headed straight for the bookshelf, where the almost-finished romance novel beckoned.

Curling up in the den on my plush couch, I

immersed myself in the world of love and fantasy. The characters danced across the pages, their passion and longing mirroring the complexities of my heart. The romantic escapade provided a temporary escape from the magical intricacies of my reality.

As afternoon turned to evening, I found comfort in the rhythmic turning of pages, losing track of time in the embrace of the fictional love affair. But reality tugged at the edges of my consciousness, reminding me of the unfinished potion that awaited my attention.

Setting the novel aside, I gathered the necessary ingredients for the dark-eye removal potion. I meticulously measured each component, whispered incantations, and stirred the concoction with care. But there was only so much I could do with my limited knowledge, and frustration crept in as the potion resisted perfection.

"Fuck!" I whisper-yelled. The nightmares were bad enough. I didn't need proof of them showing up under my tired eyes.

The cauldron emitted faint wisps of smoke, and the aroma of herbs and potions filled the air. Despite my best efforts, the potion stubbornly refused to take the desired form. It was as if the potion had a mind of its own, resisting my every effort to bring it to fruition.

With a reluctant acceptance, I decided to call it a

night for my potion-making endeavors. The disappointment lingered, but I knew when to concede defeat. Cleaning up the remnants of my failed attempts, I blew air from between clenched teeth.

Leaving the alchemical tools behind, I returned to my quiet corner with a worn book in hand. The soft glow of a nearby lamp illuminated the pages as I sank back into the world of words and stories. The comforting familiarity of the book helped me let go of the frustration that had accompanied my failed potion-making attempts.

————

The dim light of dawn filtered through my curtains, casting a pale glow on the unfinished potion sitting on the kitchen counter. Despite my best efforts the previous night, I couldn't master the intricacies of the dark-eye removal elixir. Frustration clung to me like a stubborn enchantment, and I couldn't shake the sense of inadequacy that whispered in the recesses of my mind. I traced the delicate swirls of the cauldron with my fingertips, lost in contemplation.

The truth lingered beneath the surface of my magical endeavors—I lacked the formal training that should have guided me through the complexities of spell-casting and potion brewing. My magical education had come to an abrupt halt when I was only 14. Thalia's family had stepped in, offering me a haven after my own home had become a distant memory.

The FrostFelt Werecat Clan had embraced me, providing warmth and support, but the intricacies of my magical abilities remained a puzzle that even they couldn't solve. The Werecats were skilled in their own right, but my unique magical heritage required a specialized form of guidance.

A soft sigh escaped me as I acknowledged the gap in my magical education. My journey thus far had been unconventional, marked by tragedy. Thalia's family had become my own, but Werecats did not possess the magic that Witches did.

As the morning light grew stronger, I turned away from the failed potion and ventured into the living room. The romance novel lay abandoned on the coffee table, its pages filled with the tales of love and enchantment that seemed to elude me in reality. As I ambled towards the couch, a soft thud resonated through the walls and caught my attention.

Curiosity piqued, I approached the peephole of my front door, peering into the dimly lit hallway. To my surprise, the door across the hall was ajar, and the light from a lamp danced within. My eyes widened as I glimpsed a tall figure moving about. Intrigued, I quietly stepped into the hallway, my footsteps muffled on the carpet.

As I approached, the door swung open and revealed a man with tousled chestnut hair and dark, almost black, eyes that sparkled with a warmth that seemed to defy the chilly morning. His features were sharp, and there was an air of mystery about him that made my heart skip a beat.

"Sorry to bother you. I heard a noise and thought I'd check it out. I'm Iris, I live in the apartment across the hall." I reached out my hand.

"Hello there," he greeted me with a friendly smile, his voice a soothing melody. "I'm Isaac Thorne, your new neighbor."

Isaac Thorne's smile did little to dispel the chill that traveled up my spine when we shook hands. His fingers were cold, unnaturally so, as if frost had touched him. A fleeting sensation, but one that lingered in my mind as I left him to continue settling into his new home.

Leaving Isaac with the remnants of cardboard boxes and the grating of furniture being rearranged, I retreated to my apartment. The allure of the mysterious neighbor across the hall left me curious, the enigma of this new, handsome neighbor. I closed the door behind me, and the familiar comfort of my space embraced me. I plopped on the couch, ready to finally finish my book. Feeling my phone buzz, I saw a text from Thalia.

I'm covering for Sawyer at Vulture today. Sorry I didn't text back last night, I'm still working on rearranging the schedules. Wanna come hang on my lunch break? At noon.

I checked the time, 10:45 am. *Sure,* I replied. *Should I bring lunch or do you want to go grab something together?*

I waited while she typed.

We can eat at the cafeteria inside! I don't think I'll have enough time to do a restaurant lunch.

Can do! See you at noon, kitty cat. I exchanged the phone for my book, desperate to finish the last chapter.

It was over too soon, and I closed the cover softly. I opened up my book counter app and marked it off, then checked my 'to read' list. *'Breath of Romance', available wherever books are sold.* I made a mental note to shop around after lunch with Thalia.

"Time to get ready," I attempted to motivate myself.

I shivered as I glanced out the window, the chilly embrace of the day clear with the trees waving erratically in the wind. My wardrobe presented an array of choices, but I settled on a simple yet elegant ensemble —a chunky-knit cream-colored sweater, paired with dark jeans that hugged my form comfortably. The chill in the air prompted me to add a navy scarf, a cozy accessory that would shield me from the biting wind outside.

The mirror reflected a version of myself that felt both familiar and ready for the day's adventures. I ran a brush through my long, brown hair, letting the loose waves cascade down my shoulders. A touch of makeup, subtle yet enhancing, completed the look. My blue-gray eyes critiqued the outfit, and I grabbed an oversized black wool coat to layer on top.

My thoughts drifted to the unfinished potion from the previous night, but I pushed it aside, choosing to focus on the day ahead. With a quick scan of the apartment to ensure I hadn't forgotten anything, I slung my bag over my shoulder and headed towards the door.

The brisk air greeted me as I stepped outside the apartment complex, and I tightened my coat around my lithe form, grateful for its protection against the chill. I pulled up a map on my phone and groaned when I saw how far it was from the apartment.

I walked over to the bike rack and unlocked my old moped. No one bothered to steal it. Honestly, I always felt shocked when it started up. I had found it near a dumpster when I was fifteen. Ewan and Thalia had fixed it up for me as a sixteenth birthday present.

Probably when my fascination with him started, I blushed at the memory.

I put the key in the ignition and crossed my fingers, sighing with relief when the engine sputtered to life. The city streets embraced me as I rode, the wind whipping through my hair as the moped zipped through the urban landscape.

My destination loomed ahead—an imposing structure marked with the insignia of 'Vulture Network Services'. The building stood tall and sleek, a testament to the rapid advancements within its walls. I parked my moped near the entrance; the helmet clutched in one hand as I surveyed the bustling scene.

Employees clad in professional attire hurried in and out, lost in the rhythm of their workday. As I approached the front desk, I spotted Thalia engrossed in her work. Her gaze focused on the computer screen. She didn't notice me at first. A mischievous smile played on my lips as I approached quietly. I waited for the opportune moment, then playfully tapped the desktop. Thalia looked up, her eyes widening in mock-surprise before breaking into a grin.

"Well, well, look who dropped by," she teased, the familiar warmth of her presence filling the space.

"Just thought I'd add a touch of magic to your workday," I replied with a wink.

"Give me a minute for my replacement to take over, then we can eat in the building cafeteria," Thalia said. "You can go sit in the waiting area."

The atmosphere shifted abruptly as I backed away from Thalia's workstation. In a twist of cruel fate, I found myself on a collision course with none other than Adrian Grayson.

Shit.

FOUR

A startled gasp escaped me, and I took a step back, my cheeks flushing with embarrassment. The memory of our earlier encounter at the café flooded my mind.

"Yet another smooth entrance," he remarked, his tone dripping with disdain. The words, though familiar, stung with renewed intensity. Surprised, I mumbled an apology, the weight of my awkwardness hanging in the air.

Adrian, seemingly unimpressed, looked at me with a stony expression. "What are you even doing here?"

"I'm bringing lunch to your security guard. Is there a problem with that?" I mustered a subpar retort, and gave a mocking smile.

Adrian studied me for a moment, and I held my breath. "You're much prettier when your smile is real."

Before I could reply, a voice cut through the tension like a blade. "Everything all right, sir?"

Thalia's older brother, Ewan, emerged from the nearby elevator, his presence commanding attention. Tall and confident, he exuded an air of authority that demanded respect. My heart skipped a beat as I recognized him—the same Ewan who had left me flustered countless times in the past.

Adrian's gaze shifted from me to Ewan, and a smirk played on his lips. "Just a minor mishap. Your friend here has a talent for making grand entrances," he said, his words laced with sarcasm.

Ewan, ever the diplomat, extended a hand toward Adrian. "Apologies for any inconvenience. My *sister's* friend can be a bit... enthusiastic."

My face burned with embarrassment as Ewan's words hung in the air. Thalia's brother, with his chiseled features and confident demeanor, had effortlessly turned the situation into a form of social diplomacy. I fumbled for words, attempting to salvage my dignity.

"No harm done," Adrian replied, his smirk lingering. "Just a bit of morning excitement." He took one last look at me before he strode out of the building, his phone to his ear.

The exchange left me feeling like an inconsequential pawn in a game of social dynamics. Thalia's brother, oblivious to the internal turmoil, offered a polite nod to Adrian before turning his attention to me.

"What was that all about?" He asked me bluntly.

Ewan's direct question remained between us, and I fumbled for words to articulate the embarrassing encounter with Adrian Grayson.

"It's just... I ran into him at the coffee shop the other day, and then I almost ran into him again just now. Clumsy, I know," I admitted, a nervous laugh escaping my lips.

Ewan's brow furrowed, a curiosity in his intense gaze. "Adrian Grayson? You know him from the coffee shop?"

I nodded, feeling him out. "Yeah, he was there the other morning, and we had a little collision. Now this... It's like fate is conspiring against my coordination skills."

Ewan chuckled, the sound deep and resonant, making me weak in the knees. "Fate can be a tricky thing. Maybe it's trying to tell you something.

"Or maybe," he continued, his tone lightening, "it's just a series of amusing coincidences. Either way, don't let it get to you too much."

I nodded, grateful for his reassurance. "Thanks, Ewan. It's just one of those days, I guess."

I looked at Thalia. "Ready?"

The Werecat nodded with amusement at my

exchange with her brother. "Lunch waits for no one!"
She gestured dramatically and stood.

Turning to Ewan she said, "I'll be back in an
hour."

He nodded and took her place at the desk. "See
you around, Iris," he offered.

"Oh! Uh–yeah. Bye, Ewan." I stuttered out.

Thalia linked her arm to mine and led me to the
cafeteria. Her laughter resonated, a melodic sound that
lifted my spirits. "Well, that's one way to make an
impression."

I rolled my eyes, playfully nudging her. "You know
how I am with my impressions. Always a spectacle."

Thalia's grin widened, and she squeezed my arm
affectionately. "That's why I love you, enchantress. Life
would be dull without your flair for the dramatic."

Thalia and I strolled side by side, our footsteps
echoing through the sleek corridors of the building.
The walls adorned with minimalist artwork and large
glass panels created an atmosphere of modernity. I
caught glimpses of employees engrossed in their work,
huddled in collaborative spaces with state-of-the-art
equipment.

The cafeteria doors whooshed open before us,
revealing a multitude of culinary options. Thalia
guided me to a corner table, a secluded spot close to
the windows. We settled into our seats, the hum of

conversation and the clatter of trays provided a backdrop to our lunchtime retreat. Thalia, always attuned to the nuances of my mood, steered the conversation toward lighter topics.

"Finish that romance book yet?" She asked. "I know how much you enjoy your smut." She batted her eyes next to me playfully.

"As a matter of fact, I did! On to the next, kitty cat. Want to check out the bookstore with me when you're off?"

She took a huge bite of the sandwich I had brought her and dabbed the corners of her mouth with a nearby napkin. "How about tomorrow? I don't have work until 2."

"I guess I can wait until tomorrow..." I feigned tears. "How will I survive a night without something new to read?"

Thalia balled up her napkin and tossed it at me. "Oh, the horror!"

We both laughed hard, drawing the attention of a few of Thalia's co-workers that were sitting nearby. I let my hair fall in front of my face, slightly embarrassed. I glanced out the window for a moment and noticed Adrian walking back towards the building. He was still on his phone, but he seemed to be laughing.

He has a great smile; I thought. *I can see why he's so popular with women. Didn't he tell me earlier I was pretty?* I blushed and shook my head to clear it. *I don't care.*

—————

I left the office building, the crisp air a refreshing contrast to the controlled climate inside. Retrieving my moped from its parking spot, I navigated through the city streets toward my apartment complex. Two blocks away, my gaze was drawn to my mysterious new neighbor, who was engaged in a conversation with the owner of a high-end local restaurant. Their exchange was animated, but both parties looked untroubled.

Deciding not to linger, I continued toward my apartment. Once inside, I kicked off my shoes and opened a bottle of wine, pouring myself a glass. The evening sun filtered through the curtains, casting a warm hue across the room. I settled onto the couch and scrolled through the endless options on my streaming service.

My gaze wandered to the small white bookshelf in the corner, adorned with familiar titles and well-loved novels. Even though I had promised Thalia a book date for tomorrow, I couldn't shake the yearning for a new story, a fresh escape into the realms of fantasy and romance.

Adrian Grayson's presence loomed in my

thoughts, a perplexing enigma that stirred conflicting feelings. His charisma was undeniable, and despite my reservations, there was an inexplicable allure that drew me in. But my rational side recoiled at the idea of being enamored by a reputed womanizer, a perception that clouded any potential attraction.

And then there was Ewan. I'd been attracted to him for years, and even though he could be standoffish at times, his kindness never faltered. Not that he had ever indicated I existed to him outside of being Thalia's best friend.

I swirled the wine in my glass, the dual pull of emotions left me unsettled. I shivered, and I wrapped a throw blanket around myself, seeking solace in its fuzzy embrace. The characters in my favorite novels seemed to mock my predicament, their fictional lives devoid of the complications that mirrored my own. I had had a few serious relationships here and there, but nothing ever seemed to last. Unlike Thalia, I wasn't hopeful I would find myself fated at the upcoming ball. Based on my luck, I wasn't hopeful I would ever find my fated.

Finding your fated wasn't exactly rare, but it was uncommon. It was even less common to find them with someone from a different Occult. Thalia's cousin was fated with a Harpy a few years ago, and it was all the Clan could talk about for months. The semi-annual balls that Thalia's dad liked to host boasted many fated love connections that had been made.

Stop wasting your energy thinking about guys who wouldn't give you a second thought, I chastised myself.

The weight of my heritage, a legacy steeped in magic and fated unions, bore down on me as I reflected on the story of my parents. They had been fated mates, a coupling believed to produce offspring of exceptional power. It was a theory whispered among the Occult community, a myth that suggested children born from fated unions held a unique and potent magic within them.

Thalia and Ewan were proof to others that the myth was, in fact, true. Their fated parents had definitely produced exceptional offspring. Yet, as I pondered my existence, I couldn't discern any extraordinary power coursing through my veins.

The reminiscence led my thoughts down a darker path, a labyrinth of regret and longing. My training, once a promising journey into the depths of magical mastery, had stagnated since the tender age of fourteen. The tragedy that befell my parents had not only left a void in my heart, but had also robbed me of a crucial piece of my magical heritage—the family grimoire.

Without the grimoire, a sacred tome passed down through generations, witches and warlocks were left with a void in their magical education. The intricate spells, the ancient incantations, the secrets of the craft —all locked within the pages of the grimoire. Each practitioner received their own grimoire upon reaching the age of twenty-five, a milestone that marked the completion of their training and the expansion of their magical repertoire. But here I stood, aged 27, bereft of the guiding wisdom of my family's grimoire.

I finished the last sip of wine, the rich, velvety taste leaving a lingering warmth in my chest. The plush couch cushions cradled me as I indulged in the guilty pleasure of a trashy reality TV show that Thalia and I loved to hate. The mindless drama unfolded on the screen, and I sank deeper into the couch cushions.

The absurdity of the show provided a welcome reprieve from my magical predicament and the tangled emotions of attraction that lingered in my thoughts. The minutes slipped away, and before I knew it, the TV remote had slipped from my grasp, tumbling to the floor in a soft thud. The hypnotic allure of the screen gave way to the gentle embrace of sleep, and I succumbed to the weariness that had accumulated throughout the day.

———

Shadows danced in the recesses of my mind. A hooded figure, shrouded in darkness, emerged, almost floating above the kitchen floor. The figure's sharp teeth gleamed in the dim light, each glistening with a macabre sheen. I tried to retreat, to escape the clutches of the hooded nightmare, but my movements were sluggish, as if wading through a pool of thick fog. The metallic scent of blood permeated the air, and the figure's teeth dripped with crimson ichor. The figure lunged at me with menace, its movements swift and predatory.

FIVE

With a jolt I awoke on the couch, gasping for breath as the dregs of the nightmare lingered in the recesses of my consciousness. The reality TV show had long ended, the room now shrouded in the quiet stillness of the early morning. The wine glass stood empty on the coffee table, and I ran my tongue over my unbrushed teeth and grimaced.

It was just a nightmare, I reassured myself. *If they haven't come for you after all this time, then they're not going to.*

———

The remnants of the nightmare clung to the corners of my consciousness, making the prospect of returning to sleep a distant hope. In the hushed stillness of the early morning, I embraced the solitude and cleared my head with a brisk jog. The chilly hardwood floor bit at my skin as I hastily dressed, slipping into activewear to combat the morning coolness.

The city was slowly awakening; the streets adorned with the soft glow of streetlights that painted a serene picture against the predawn sky. As I jogged through the quiet neighborhoods, the rhythmic patter of my footsteps became a comforting cadence, drowning out the echoes of the unsettling dream that lingered in my thoughts.

I marveled at the tranquility of the morning, the crisp air invigorating my senses as I navigated the familiar paths that crisscrossed the landscape. Each stride was a deliberate motion, a dance with the awakening city that offered a sense of clarity amidst the lingering shadows of the night.

The streets were gradually coming to life, and I noticed the subtle beauty in the architecture of the houses I passed. Vines cascaded down wrought-iron fences, adding a touch of wild elegance to the suburbia. The city was gradually waking up, and I couldn't help but appreciate the contrast between the urban hustle and the tranquility of the early hour. It felt good to sweat and enjoy the simple moments that adorned the morning landscape.

On the return journey to my apartment, a figure caught my eye—Isaac Thorne, my neighbor, stepped out of his door, dressed handsomely in business attire. The early morning light stressed the effortless charm that seemed to accompany him. Our paths converged, and a friendly smile played on his lips.

"Good morning, Iris," he greeted, his voice carrying a casual elegance that matched his demeanor. "Early jog to kick off the day?"

I nodded, returning the smile. "Couldn't sleep, so I figured I'd make the most of the morning."

Isaac chuckled, the sound carrying a warmth that matched the sunrise. "I can relate. Early riser myself. I find it's the perfect time to clear the mind."

As we chatted, Isaac shared a bit about himself. An angel investor for local businesses, his work involved supporting and nurturing the growth of the community. I realized I had spotted him yesterday engaged in conversation with the owner of a local restaurant, likely discussing potential investments.

The realization added a layer of intrigue to our interaction, and I found myself drawn to the charisma that seemed to radiate from Isaac.

"Well, I'd better get going. It is always a pleasure talking to you, Iris. I hope I see you again soon," he said.

His departure left me with a lingering smile as I

walked over to my unit. Returning to the warmth of my living space, I shed the layers of my morning excursion and stood beneath the rejuvenating cascade of the shower. The water washed away the rest of the unsettling dream, and the brisk chill of the morning jog.

As I stood before the mirror contemplating my reflection, a gentle knock on the door indicated Thalia's arrival. The rich aroma of coffee and the tempting scent of freshly baked scones wafted into the room as I opened the door to my best friend.

"Good morning, enchantress," Thalia greeted with a mischievous grin, holding out a steaming cup of coffee and a bag of blueberry scones. "I come bearing gifts of caffeine and carbs to start your day right."

I accepted the offerings with a grateful smile, savoring the warmth that radiated from the cup. "You're a lifesaver, kitty cat. I was just trying to figure out what I was going to make for breakfast."

Thalia chuckled, eyeing the clutter in my apartment with an amused glint in her eyes. "Iris, when was the last time you went grocery shopping? Your kitchen looks like it's in dire need of restocking."

I rolled my eyes, knowing she wasn't wrong. "Alright, alright. We can make a pit stop on our way back today."

"Deal," she agreed with a satisfied nod.

With our morning treats in hand, Thalia and I

stepped out into the cool embrace of the day. The aroma of coffee lingered as a comforting companion, and our steps fell into a rhythm as we strolled through the city.

"There are a couple of bookstores I've been meaning to check," I mentioned to Thalia, the anticipation of discovering a new read brightening my gaze. "I'm on the lookout for 'Breath of Romance'. It's been on my 'to be read' for ages."

Thalia's eyes lit up. "Oh, the one with the mysterious, brooding hero and the fiery heroine? I remember you talking about it. Maybe I'll grab one too!"

We rounded the corner, the quaint cobblestone street lined with charming old buildings. A warm glow emanated from a small storefront ahead, 'About Tome'. Something unseen pulled me towards it, and I let my legs carry me forward. The soft chime of a bell welcomed us as I opened the creaky door that announced our arrival at the cozy, local used bookstore. The scent of well-loved books, a blend of aged paper and ink, enveloped me. I breathed in deeply.

Wooden shelves stretched from floor to ceiling, filled with an eclectic array of books. Sunlight streamed through the leaded glass windows and cast a gentle glow on the worn wooden floor and inviting reading nooks. The air was filled with the hushed whispers of pages being turned and the occasional creaking of the floorboards as patrons move about.

Each section of the bookstore was meticulously curated, with hand-written recommendations and small cards peeking out from between the volumes. The friendly bookseller, perched behind an antique counter, looked up with a welcoming smile. The bookstore cat, curled up on a sunlit window sill, lazily opened one eye to acknowledge our presence before resuming its nap.

Thalia touched my shoulder, and I paused. "I totally spaced - I have work in forty-five minutes," Thalia spoke quietly to not disturb the readers. "I'll catch up with you later, yeah?"

I nodded and waved my hand, my eyes still on the rows of books. I ran my fingertips over the worn spines, feeling the texture of the paper and the history contained within each volume. And then, there it was— a book standing slightly askew on the shelf, as if it had been waiting for me.

Its cover, adorned with intricate designs, caught the glimmer of the overhead lights, casting an ethereal glow. The title, written in elegant script, seemed to whisper directly to my soul. 'Kane'.

It has to be a coincidence that my family name is on here, right? Right?

I hesitated for a moment, the connection palpable.

It was as though the book itself was extending an invitation, a beckoning call that resonated with something deep within me. The world around me blurred as I reached for the book, a thrill coursing through my veins. I held it in my hands. The weight felt just right, as if the universe had conspired to guide me to this very moment. I traced my fingers over the cover, feeling the embossed patterns beneath them. I carried the tome and walked purposefully towards the clerk.

"I don't recognize this one," the cashier mused aloud and slightly scrunched her brows. "But enjoy!"

With the book securely in my bag, I stepped back into the world outside. The afternoon chill quickly sunk into my bones, and I quickened my pace. I spy a postal box a block from home and drop the completed orders in.

Fuck, it's cold. I shivered and hugged my book tighter to my chest.

The quaint cobblestone street led me back to my apartment building, its ivy-covered facade welcoming me home. I couldn't wait to escape the biting chill of the afternoon, eager to delve into the mysterious book I had found at 'About Tome'.

The heavy wooden door to my building groaned as I pushed it open, the familiar creaks echoing through the lobby. My footsteps echoed in the narrow hallway as I climbed the worn staircase to my floor. The key turned smoothly in the lock, and the door swung open to reveal my cozy apartment, a haven from the world outside.

I kicked off my shoes and headed straight for the small bookshelf nestled in the corner, making space for the new addition. The subtle glow of the book's cover caught my eye as I placed it on top of a few worn classics and forgotten tales on the side table next to my favorite armchair.

The scent of old books mingled with the warmth of the teakettle on the stove. I wandered to the side table where my new book now rested, and its cover seemed to shimmer with an otherworldly light. With a furrowed brow, I reached for the book, tracing the embossed title with my fingertips.

I sat down and gingerly opened the strange book with my namesake on the cover. This wasn't just any book; it was the long-lost Kane family grimoire. The significance of its discovery sent shivers down my spine, and my hands trembled as I carefully opened the pages.

'Kane Family Grimoire,' I read the first page over and over again.

This can't be a coincidence. My pulse raced and my fingers trembled.

SIX

I flipped the pages slowly, trying to glean more information about the tome. The words within were a dance of ancient wisdom, a tapestry of incantations passed down through generations. The revelations within the grimoire opened a door to a world I had only glimpsed in dreams.

It spoke of a legacy intertwined with the mystical energies that flowed through Silver Grove. The stories of my ancestors became vivid tales of magic and destiny, and I found myself captivated by the untold history of the Kane family. The hours slipped away as I delved into the pages, absorbing the knowledge that had long been hidden from me. I flipped to the family tree and choked back a sob when I saw my parent's names.

Maude Kane. Deceased.

Osran Kane. Deceased.

———

In the quaint town of Silver Grove, where the whispering winds carried secrets through the ancient trees, Osran and Maude Kane lived a life filled with love and enchantment. They were a fated couple deeply connected to the magical currents that flowed through the town, their bond an echo of the mystical energies that permeated their surroundings.

Osran, with his silver-streaked hair and piercing green eyes, was a master of elemental magic, attuned to the natural forces that shaped the world around him. His days were spent tending to the family garden, coaxing vibrant blooms to life with a touch that seemed to channel the very essence of nature.

Maude, a vision of grace with her flowing auburn hair and laughter that sparkled like sunlight on a crystal-clear stream, possessed the gift of Chrono-Crafting: she could craft unique artifacts infused with temporal energy. These artifacts had various effects, such as temporarily freezing time in a small, localized area or accelerating the growth of plants. Crafting these items required a deep understanding of the temporal forces at play, and her magic was incredibly rare.

Their idyllic life took an unforeseen turn when

Maude began to feel an unnatural and ominous presence, keeping tabs on herself, Osran, and Iris. Alarmed and determined to protect their family, Osran and Maude delved into ancient texts, seeking answers to the cryptic threat that haunted them. Doing their best to protect Iris, the fourteen year old was blissfully unaware of the danger that lurked so closely to the Kane family until it was too late.

Iris came home from school one day to blood. So much blood. Osran lay in the front hall, his body too motionless to just have been unconscious. As Iris crept towards him, bile rising in her throat when she saw the upper half up his body. His chest was caved in, a hole where his heart should have been. Blood pooled around his torso, and his lifeless eyes stared at nothing.

Iris recalled stumbling to the kitchen, tears in her eyes and her stomach in turmoil. A hooded figure leaned over Maude, its face close to hers. Iris called out, and the figure looked to the young girl. The shroud concealed everything but their mouth, their white fangs dripping with Maude's crimson blood.

Her mother's throat bore marks that matched her assailant's teeth, and Iris staggered back as the being moved towards her. The last thing she remembered was screaming, and waking up in a nearby hospital surrounded by Thalia and her family. No one could explain why Iris was left alive, or what the attackers goal was. The official mortal police report stated a home invasion gone wrong, ending in arson that left the home in ashes.

With heavy hearts, Thalia's family and the Frostfelt Clan took Iris under their wing, raising her as their own alongside Thalia and Ewan. The connection between the families deepened as the girls grew up as sisters, yet the pain of Iris' loss lingered, an unspoken sorrow that wove its way into the fabric of their shared history.

———

I wiped away the tears that had escaped, which trailed down my cheeks like silent rivers. The weight of the past, the ache of a loss that time had failed to heal, stayed stuck in the edges of my heart. It had been twelve years since the day my parents were taken from me, and the specter of their killer still eluded me like a shadow in the night. The investigation had long gone cold, and the information I sought about the malevolent Occult who had torn my family apart remained frustratingly elusive.

It wasn't until my discovery of the long-lost Kane family grimoire today that a glimmer of hope pierced through the darkness. The pages, worn with age and imbued with the magic of generations past, held secrets that had long been hidden from me. Most of the incantations were inscribed in a language that seemed to dance on the edge of understanding, a cryptic code that begged to be unraveled.

I took a moment and spelled a bottle of wine and a glass over to me. The items trembled over; the magic I did know was only as good as my mental state. With a shaky hand, I wiggled the stopper out and gave myself a heavy pour. I drank deeply, almost finishing the glass in one gulp. I poured again, knocking it back once more. I poured a third time and forced myself to slow down.

I flipped through the magical tome, finally finding a thick section of English. I could feel the blood pumping in my veins, my eyes struggling to focus on anything specific. The grimoire contained basic and intermediate spells, and fueled a determination that had been dormant for far too long.

I can finally continue my training, I thought as my eyes welled with tears once again.

The answers I sought might still be buried within the intricate web of the grimoire's language, but the foundational spells would allow me to learn those answers once my skill set progressed.

But I still couldn't stop thinking about my parents. I drank deeply from my glass and stood shakily, looking for something to eat.

Damn. I was supposed to go to the grocery store on my way back home. I sighed.

I was pretty drunk, the wine on an empty stomach had me feeling more than tipsy. I weighed the option of making a quick run to the convenience store across the street, or ordering delivery. I glanced over at the open grimoire. Delivery it is.

I traced the intricate patterns on the grimoire's cover, the source of both newfound power and the ache of a void left by my parents. They were meant to be my guides, my mentors in the mystical arts. The realization that I now held the key to completing my training only amplified the longing for my family's presence, the absence of their guidance a poignant reminder of what should have been.

I polished off the rest of the wine bottle, and slowly turned the pages in the magical book. The solitude of the apartment echoed with my thoughts, the subdued lighting casting a somber ambiance.

A knock at the door disrupted the contemplative silence, signaling the arrival of my pasta delivery. With a weary sigh, I rose to answer the door, hoping the distraction would offer a reprieve from the emotional storm.

As I swung the door open, the aroma of fresh Italian food wafted in, mingling with the lingering scent of the wine. To my surprise, Isaac stood on the other side, returning home from work. His presence added an unexpected twist to the day, his gaze meeting mine with a warmth that momentarily eased the shadows in my heart.

"Hey there," he greeted, a smile playing on his lips. "That smells delicious."

"Isaac," I murmured, my feet seeming to move on their own accord towards my handsome neighbor.

My fingers gently grazed the nape of his neck, tracing along the sinewy contours of his physique, my touch lingering upon his firm biceps and sculpted chest. Isaac turned his gaze towards me, his expression curious, but interested. With a swift motion, he grasped my hand, pulling me closer until our bodies merged into one, our lips mere inches apart.

His scent, a heady blend of vetiver and musk, filled my nostrils, sending waves of arousal coursing through my veins. "I hoped you would come to me," he murmured, his breath warm against her ear. "I could feel the electricity between us every time we crossed paths."

Isaac's lips curled into a knowing smile. His hand traced down my bare arm, causing goosebumps to rise up on my skin. He quickly unlocked his door, and looked at me invitingly. "Shall we?" He smiled.

Fuck it, I thought. *I* need *this.*

Isaac wrapped his arms around me, pressing his

chiseled body firmly against mine. My lips parted slightly, our tongues intertwined. My hands roamed freely, exploring every inch of flesh beneath my fingertips. Isaac cupped my face, kissing me deeply, his tongue dancing with mine. I moaned softly, arching my back as his hands slid down my waist, caressing my hips and thighs.

"You're so beautiful," Isaac murmured, his voice husky with lust.

His fingers danced across the delicate lace of my bra, teasing my nipples with gentle flicks and pinches. I whimpered softly, my body leaning into his touch. I took a deep breath, gathering my courage.

"I want you," I said, my voice cracking slightly. "I want to feel your hands all over my body."

Isaac smirked, his black eyes sparkling with mischief. "Oh, sweetheart," he breathed, reaching out to trace his index finger along my cheekbone. "You have no idea how much I want to do that."

As he spoke, his hand slid beneath the lace of my bra, cupping my breast and squeezing gently. I gasped, my breath hitching at the sensation. Isaac's fingers trailed down my side, skimming lightly over my hip, and then began to tug my jeans down, exposing my toned legs and the pale satin triangle of my panties. His breath quickened, and he lowered his mouth to my collarbone, sucking gently at my sensitive skin.

I watched as Isaac removed his shirt, revealing his chiseled chest and toned abs. His muscles rippled beneath his skin, and I bit my lip. As he undid his belt and allowed his pants to fall to the floor, his erection jutted forth. I felt his hardness press against my thigh, and a wave of heat surged through my body.

I wanted him, needed him, craved him. Isaac unfastened my bra with ease. As he slipped it off, he stared at my exposed breasts, his gaze burning with desire. Isaac smiled wickedly, his eyes shining with lustful intent. He guided me to the plush leather couch, where he pulled me on top of him. I ran my nails down his arms and chest, and he shivered with desire.

His hands explored my body, mapping every curve and contour with expert precision. He leaned forward, his lips grazing the hollow of my throat. I shivered, and tried not to shy away from his dominance. His hands roamed lower, tugging off my jeans. As he pulled them down, I lifted my hips, allowing him easier access.

"Good girl," he murmured, his voice thick with lust.

He switched positions with me, and admired the way my body responded to his ministrations, my nipples erect and my breathing labored. He reached down, slipping his fingers beneath the waistband of my underwear, and tugged them away.

As soon as they fell to the ground, he leaned in,

kissing my inner thigh. I gasped, my knees buckling slightly. Isaac's lips traveled upwards, kissing and tasting the skin around my labia. His tongue swirled around my clit, eliciting a moan that echoed throughout the room.

My heart pounded wildly in my chest, and my palms grew clammy with anticipation. I nodded, my voice barely audible. "Yes," I whispered.

SEVEN

My body writhed beneath his attention, my hips bucking involuntarily. Isaac's fingers delved deeper, probing my wet depths, seeking purchase within me. I cried out, my voice rising in pitch as I neared the precipice.

"I need to be inside you," Isaac growled, his voice low and urgent.

He shifted position, kneeling between my legs. His erection jutted forth, throbbing with an insatiable hunger. My breath caught in my throat. He was huge. Isaac had positioned himself between my legs, his powerful thighs framing my delicate form. I watched as he tore open the condom wrapper and slid it on his length.

He reached down, gently parting my legs with his muscular thighs. I felt the cool air brush against my most intimate regions, making me shiver. Isaac placed his hands on either side of me, his palms resting on the couch cushions.

His hands rested on my hips, holding me steady as he prepared to enter me. His cockhead breached my tight opening, stretching my flesh. I gasped, my body convulsing with pain and pleasure. He continued to push, his cock sliding deeper, filling me with his length. I moaned loudly, my body writhing beneath him.

I took a deep breath, my chest rising and falling in sync with my rapidly beating heart. He pushed further, his cock sliding deeper within me, stretching my tight passage with each inward thrust. I could feel the sweat dripping from his brow, staining my skin, mingling with my own perspiration.

His movements became more frantic, punctuated by grunts and moans that reverberated through the small apartment. He plunged deeper, thrusting harder, his cock filling me to the brim.

"Fuck," he groaned. "I'm almost at my limit."

I cried out, but it was muffled by his lips, as he crushed mine with a desperate kiss. He thrust upward, burying himself deep within me, feeling my walls contract around his shaft. Isaac gripped my hips, his fingers digging into my flesh. His thrusts became more forceful, relentless, as if trying to conquer me completely.

"That's it, baby," Isaac growled, his voice thick with lust.

Isaac grinned wickedly, his cock sliding effortlessly in and out. His cock swelled within me, and he let out a deep moan as he came.

We collapsed onto the couch together, breathless and spent. Our bodies slick with sweat and tangled in a passionate embrace. We lay there, our ragged breaths mingling, hearts pounding in time with one another.

Isaac smiled confidently, his eyes shining with lustful intent. "I'm sure you enjoyed that as much as I did."

His confidence was a turn on, and the sex did exactly what I had hoped it would - take my mind off of the grimoire, and the sadness of remembering what had happened to my parents. But our sexual escapade had ended, and all of the sweating we did had significantly lessened the effects of the wine. I must have had a faraway look on my face, because Isaac coughed politely.

"Let me take you out to a proper dinner tomorrow. There's this fantastic new restaurant I've been just dying to try. What do you say?"

"I'd love to, but I have some work I need to finish

before the weekend," I declined kindly, thinking about the grimoire.

I thought I saw fury in his dark eyes, but when I blinked, I only saw polite disappointment.

"How about Saturday?" He asked.

The invitation hung in the air, and I'll admit a flicker of excitement ignited within me. "That sounds great," I replied, a smile playing on my lips. "Stop by at eight?"

"Excellent," Isaac smiled.

Putting our clothes back on was not nearly as fun as taking them off, but Isaac had an early following day. Our lips brushed tenderly before he closed the door, and I walked back to my own unit, pulling out my phone.

Thalia, are you still up? I found something important.

You know I am! What's up? The Werecat quickly replied.

I'm coming over. This can't wait.

??? Was Thalia's reply.

But I was already out the door, bracing myself against the frigidity of the night, my eyes scanning the bike rack for my shitty moped. The wind cut through the air as I zipped along the narrow path that led to the outskirts of Silver Grove.

The chill bit at my cheeks, but the rhythmic motion of the bike beneath me, coupled with the adrenaline of anticipation, kept me warm. The familiar sights of the town, with its cobblestone streets and charming storefronts, gradually gave way to the outskirts where the secrets of the Occult were veiled by a mortal façade.

The imposing iron gates, guarded by vigilant sentinels of stone statues, marked the threshold between the bustling city and the concealed quarters of the FrostFelt Werecat Clan. Tudor-style homes lined the streets, and soft pools of light emanated from the wrought-iron street lamps, casting a warm glow that danced upon the cobblestone pathways.

I typed in the code and the gate creaked open, revealing a path that meandered through the expansive grounds. The crisp air carried the scent of pine and frost, a testament to the magical aura that enveloped the Clan's territory. Riding through the picturesque landscape, I marveled at the illusion my parents had crafted to keep the Clan's existence concealed from the prying eyes of mortal neighbors.

I approached Thalia's family home, nestled in the heart of the Clan's territory. The architecture blended seamlessly with the surrounding woods, an elegant synthesis of nature and craftsmanship. I dismounted my moped and walked to the door. The unmistakable and familiar scent of pine needles and wintergreen permeated the air.

Thalia greeted me with a warm smile as she opened the door, her yellow eyes gleaming with the unmistakable luminescence of her Werecat lineage.

"Iris, you're here! Why do you smell like sex? Come in, it's freezing out there."

We settled in her family's cozy living room, the flickering fire in the hearth casting a comforting glow. In the safety of the neighborhood, Thalia allowed some of her more feline traits to manifest, and I marveled at her Saffron cat ears that swiveled to even the most minute of sounds.

She padded over to me and gestured to the plush living room couch. Over mugs of steaming tea, I shared the revelation of the Kane family grimoire and the newfound training I had embarked upon. Thalia listened intently, tugging at her necklace. Her feline ears twitched with curiosity, and her vertical pupils ebbed and flowed as she absorbed the details of my earlier discovery.

"The FrostFelt Werecat Clan has its own share of ancient spells and lore," Thalia mused. "I can request the elders for access to the library."

"That would be great!" I opened the grimoire and handed it to my best friend. "See these large sections of text? I've never seen anything like it before. Maybe the FrostFelt archives will know more," I said hopefully.

Thalia studied the book and nodded. "Do you think the grimoire might have more information about this amulet? I've always wondered about it. I got it from my grandmother when she passed away when I was nine. She was adamant in her will that I receive it, I'd love to know more."

"It's worth a try," I replied. "The family grimoire is a repository of generations' worth of magical knowledge. If there's anything magical about this amulet, it would likely be within those pages. But what about the archives? Did you already ask the elders about it?"

"I got it when I was so young, and I wasn't thinking about stuff like that. But I've been wearing it every day since it was given to me, and almost forgot about the mysteries it may hold. Until today, that is," she added.

"Maybe the archives will have the answers we *both* want," I said. "But in the meantime, we can definitely check the book."

The fire crackled, casting dancing shadows on the walls. "Thank you, enchantress." Thalia smiled. "Now that I have the scheduling figured out for our warriors to help the DuskHeart Clan, I have the archives to attend to, and the upcoming ball to focus on." Despite her exhaustion, Thalia's eyes lit up at the mention of the ball.

"You won't believe how much my dad has loosened up about the guest list this year," Thalia bubbled with enthusiasm. "He's finally opened it up to all Occults in Silver Grove, *and* the surrounding towns."

I raised my eyebrows. "All Occults? That's a big change. Who's going to be there?"

"We aren't allowed access to the guest list until my dad decides we're ready to handle that kind of privileged information." She rolled her eyes.

"But I can say that there'll be Werecats, but there will also be some prominent Covens, and even small shifter Clans made up of other animal shifters. Oh, and the nymphs, too. Now *they* know how to party." Thalia's silky tail flicked with excitement.

"There might be even more Occults showing up at the last minute. You know how these things go. Sometimes, a few unexpected guests decide to grace us with their presence. Is your mystery bootycall Occult?"

"He seems mortal to me," I said. "But I wouldn't invite him, anyway! We haven't even had a date yet. I still need to see if there's a spark emotionally, too, you know?"

Thalia nodded, and her tone turned serious. "My parents pulled me aside after Clan dinner this evening. If I don't find my fated at this ball, my dad has been dropping not-so-subtle hints about arranging a marriage of alliance. The WickedFang Clan is powerful, and the melding of our dynasties would be beneficial to everyone - except me."

The idea of an arranged marriage seemed like a relic from a bygone era, yet the weight of tradition and the expectations of our Occult society bore down on the prospect.

"I don't want to see you forced into anything, Thalia," I reassured her, my gray-blue eyes reflecting the sincerity of my concern. "But if there's one place to find your fated, it's at the ball. And you'll have me by your side all night."

EIGHT

Morning sunlight filtered through the curtains, casting a gentle glow on the living room of Thalia's family's house. I stirred on the plush couch, the familiar scent of pine and wintergreen always lingering in the air. A quiet yawn escaped my lips as I stretched, the reality of a new day settling in. The warmth of the flickering fireplace offered a stark contrast to the chill that clung to the outside.

Thalia, with her saffron cat ears perked, entered the room, a knowing smile playing on her lips. "Good morning, sleepyhead. Ready for some magic today?"

Rubbing the sleep from my eyes, I nodded emphatically. The grimoire lay entangled in my blankets, its cover shimmering as if aware of the secrets it held. Thalia joined me, her yellow eyes shining. I grabbed the grimoire from beside myself. I must have been holding it in my sleep.

"Let's start with the basics, and test my skill level first. I have learned nothing new since I was fourteen. Before my parents–" I choked a little on the last sentence.

Thalia padded over and wrapped her arms around me. "I know, Iris. It's okay. Let's just start small."

We separated, and she took the grimoire from my hands. "Lets, see... I know you already know how to do basic levitation, but how about conjuring?"

Thalia guided me through the incantation, her voice a steady rhythm. The words danced on the edge of familiarity, a melody that echoed with ancient wisdom. Focusing on the words, I felt a subtle energy stir within me, responding to the call of the spell.

"Concentrate, Iris. Feel the surrounding magic," Thalia encouraged, her eyes fixed on mine.

I closed my eyes, taking a deep breath. The room hummed with a subtle energy, and I recited the incantation and envisioned the spell taking shape. Slowly, half of my favorite mug from back at my apartment appeared in my outstretched hands.

Thalia covered her mouth, snickering. "Well... You have to start somewhere."

I gave her a dirty look, but couldn't stop myself from laughing as well. Every time we tried to return to the spell, one of us would take one look at the half-mug and lose it again.

"Okay, okay," I said, wiping the tears from my eyes. "Let's get the rest of this mug over here so I can fill it with that expensive coffee your mom likes."

I cleared my mind, and concentrated on the new spell. Chanting quietly, I imagined the other half of the mug. It appeared in my outstretched hand.

Emboldened by the success, we delved into a few more elementary spells, each one a step deeper into the mystical tapestry of the grimoire. The air crackled with magic, a dance between the mundane and the extraordinary. With each success, my confidence increased exponentially. I wiped the sweat from my brow with my sleep shirt and sat down on the living room rug, my body too tired to continue.

"Let's take a break," I mumbled to my friend. "I think I'm gonna head back home to work on some more orders that came in this morning. I'm all magicked out for now." I gave her a tired smile.

Thalia reached for her phone, her fingers dancing over the screen as she composed a message. "Requesting access to the FrostFelt Clan library archives," Thalia murmured as she typed. "Sent. You go home. I'll reach out when I get a reply."

I stood, and Thalia handed me my grimoire. "Love you, kitty cat," I said, as I walked out the front door.

She audibly purred. "Love you, enchantress. I'll be helping my mom with Clan paperwork until this evening, but I'll be by this evening after I fix your mug." She laughed again.

"And I should have more info on the ball!" She blew me a kiss and closed the door.

———

The sun was high in the midafternoon sky, casting long shadows across the cobblestone streets of Silver Grove as I revved up my moped. The frigid wind stung my cheeks, but the rhythmic hum of the engine beneath me and the promise of new spells in the Kane family grimoire tucked safely in my bag fueled me.

A sudden craving for a pick-me-up tugged at my senses, and I steered my moped towards the small establishment. 'Divine Bliss Espresso' stood like a beacon on the corner.

The door chimed as I entered, the friendliness of the café enveloping me like a comforting embrace. The low hum of hushed conversations and the rhythmic whirr of the espresso machine filled the air. I approached the counter, greeted by the barista's friendly smile.

"One Americano to go, please," I requested.

I scanned the room while I waited, and there, in a

corner booth, sat Adrian Grayson. His sage button-down contrasting perfectly against his russet eyes. His presence, as enigmatic as ever, drew my gaze. He glanced up from his computer, his piercing gaze meeting mine. There was something magnetic about the way his eyes held mine. I nodded slightly to the man and tried not to let my blush show.

"No accidental run-ins today?" he quipped.

I took a few steps towards him and stopped. "Well, the day is still young," I retorted. "I can only hope the next person will be as understanding as you were." I crossed my arms.

The normally aloof man looked embarrassed for a second, and he ruffled his brown hair. "I can be a bit harsh at times. Accidents can happen. Even twice in a row."

My eyes widened at his semi-apology, and before I responded, he spoke again. "I'm Adrian. Adrian Grayson. And you are?"

"I'm—"

"8 oz Americano for Iris?" The barista called out.

"That's me." I grabbed my drink and turned back to the suave man. "Until next time," I said, a smile tugging at the corners of my lips.

"Until next time, Iris," Adrian replied, his remarkable eyes crinkling in amusement. My toes curled at the way his deep voice said my name, and I tried not to let it show as I walked to the front of the shop. I could feel Adrian's eyes on me, a silent exchange that left me both intrigued and oddly satisfied.

I pushed the door and unlocked my transportation quickly, while still keeping my drink upright. I slid the coffee in the cupholder and turned the key in the ignition - the moped sputtering to life beneath me. Speeding away, the mysterious connection with Silver Grove's bad boy lingered like the steam rising from the cup in my cup holder.

———

The hum of my moped echoed through the narrow streets as I approached my apartment complex. As I parked and walked towards the entrance, a figure leaned casually against the building, holding their phone. Isaac Thorne greeted me with a charming smile.

"Good evening, Iris," he said, his voice a velvet melody that sent a shiver down my spine.

"Hi Isaac," I replied with a soft smile.

Isaac's gaze lingered on me, his eyes holding a magnetic allure. "I was just heading out to grab a bite. Care to join me?"

His invitation hung in the air. As tempted as I was, my body sagged with exhaustion from my earlier magical training. "I've had a long day, I can barely hold my eyes open. Sorry, Isaac."

His dark eyes slanted, and I took an unconscious step back. Just as swiftly as it had happened; Isaac's demeanor shifted rapidly, and returned to the familiar kindness and softness that I was accustomed to.

"No worries, Iris," he said coolly. "Just as long as we're still on for tomorrow?" I was still feeling strange from his previous expression, but when he gave me a soft smile, I couldn't help but smile back.

"I wouldn't miss it," I said.

I pulled out my phone as I climbed the stairs to my floor, opening up a thread between Thalia and I.

You will never guess the day I've had after I left your place, I sent.

I walked up to my door, my keys jingling against the handle as I twisted the knob and pushed my way inside. The coffee had given me a much needed energy boost, and I said a quick and familiar enchantment to turn on all of the lights in the living room and kitchen.

I'm on my way, Thalia finally replied.

I brought the grimoire over to the kitchen island and opened it to one of the spells from this morning. I allowed the words to form in my mind, their cadence a rhythmic dance echoing in the corridors of my consciousness. The air crackled with energy, a subtle transformation that hinted at the spell taking shape.

I opened my eyes to witness a manifestation of magic—the teapot on the stove began to gently whistle, steam rising in a graceful dance. It was a simple spell, yet the sense of accomplishment swelled within me. I turned my attention to the front door now, where the knob twisted and then was pushed open by a smiling Thalia.

"Why do you smell like two different males?" She grinned mischievously and her features became even more feline than usual. "And why is one of them Adrian Grayson?"

"Why do you know what Adrian Grayson smells like?" I retorted.

I just met this man, why am I getting all defensive? I chastised myself.

Thalia raised her eyebrows at me, but otherwise didn't remark on my outburst. "At the coffee shop when you ran into him. I'd recognize that scent anywhere; cashmere, cedar, and eucalyptus."

She stalked towards me and breathed deeply. "But this other scent I'm not so sure of. Vetiver and... musk? It's subtle. Wait... I totally smelled it on you the other night!"

"You're good at that!" I complemented the Werecat. "I ran into my new neighbor before I texted you. He invited me on a date tomorrow," I wiggled my eyebrows.

She walked over to the cabinets and helped herself to some biscotti and black tea bags. I conjured two mugs in front of her and she gave me a wink. I strolled to the couch and summoned the remote, tuning the tv into a random rom com for some cozy background noise.

"Enough about me for now," I said. "Do you have more info about the ball?"

Thalia brought the mugs over and sat them on the wooden coffee table. She stretched, and pulled out her tablet. "More info about the decór than I know what to do with, and I still don't have any idea on who is actually attending. My dad said it's privileged information." she complained. Oh, and the ball is two weeks from now." She rolled her eyes.

"I didn't realize it was so close!" I got up from the couch and walked to my room. "I have nothing to wear!"

"I said 'a month ago' two weeks ago, enchantress. Although life has thrown a lot our way lately," Thalia noted.

I sipped on my tea thoughtfully. "What do I need to know?"

"Well, my mom and the planner decided on 'starry night soiree,' so I'm thinking we will go all out in celestial glam. She wanted to go with 'midnight masquerade' but I managed to convince her that no one was going to find their fated hidden behind a mask."

"Well we don't have much time to find our gowns," I mused. "Shall we check the book?" I winked.

"A gown made by magic? Check the book, enchantress!"

Nine

The grimoire lay open on the kitchen island. Thalia and I were fueled by the success of our previous conjuration, and were eager to delve deeper into the mysteries woven within my grimoire's pages.

Thalia pulled out her phone and displayed a picture of a plain, black, floor length dress. "Alright, enchantress. Let's test it out. See this dress? Visualize it, every detail, every nuance. Let's bring it forth."

I nodded, my gaze fixed on the image. The challenge lay not in the unfamiliar, but in the familiar—a dress I had seen Thalia wear on various occasions, its fabric imprinted with memories. Closing my eyes, I summoned the mental image of the black dress, its silhouette and texture vivid in my imagination.

The incantation flowed from my lips, a rhythmic

dance of ancient words that resonated with the magical energies surrounding us. In the canvas of my mind, the image of the black dress stood distinctly. I wove the threads of imagination into a tangible reality, and as I opened my eyes, the living room bore witness to the manifestation of the slinky dress.

Thalia's applause filled the room, her excitement mirroring my own. The black dress hung gracefully, a testament to the potency of visualization and the grimoire's teachings.

"Let's see what else I'm capable of," I said with a grin.

I flipped through the aged pages, searching for the elusive incantation that would allow us to transfigure an item into a different form.

Thalia's eyes scanned the text alongside mine, her tail swishing with anticipation. We sound a section on basic transfiguration spells, each entry holding the promise of metamorphosis. Among them, a spell that resonated with our goal—a transfiguration that could alter the appearance of an object while retaining its fundamental essence.

I rotated my neck in a circle and stretched my limbs. "Let's begin."

———

The witching hour had long passed, and the apartment glowed with a dim, warm light as Thalia and I stood amidst the remnants of our nocturnal endeavor. The gowns, ethereal creations born from threads and incantations, now adorned the room like silent guardians of a secret pact.

Fatigue weighed heavily on my shoulders, a tangible reminder of the magical tapestry we had woven throughout the night. Thalia's cat ears drooped with weariness, mirroring the exhaustion etched on my face.

A triumphant smile tugged at the corners of my lips. "They look incredible, kitty cat. I couldn't have done it without you."

The grimoire, now closed and resting on the kitchen island, seemed to glow with satisfaction.

"Let's call it a night," I suggested, my body yearning for the comfort of my bed.

Thalia nodded, her feline grace clear even in moments of weariness. "Agreed. We've earned a good night's rest."

We tidied the rest of the fabric and sewing tools, a comforting silence settled between us. The gowns, luminescent in the lamplight, stood as a testament to the enchantment that thrived in the small hours of the morning. I slipped into my pajamas, the fatigue of the night clinging to my every step. The softness of the bed welcomed me, a sanctuary promising respite from the magical endeavors that had consumed our night.

Closing my eyes, I let out a sigh of relief. The images of spells and stitches faded, replaced by the gentle hum of the night. The grimoire, now resting on my bedside table, seemed to radiate a subtle energy—a silent guardian as dreams and enchantments danced on the edge of my consciousness.

The night had been a tapestry of haunting dreams, pulling me back into the labyrinth of memories. Shadows of my parents, the Occult assailant, and the blood-stained halls of my childhood home haunted the corners of my subconscious.

———

As I stirred on the edge of consciousness, weariness clung to me like a lingering fog. The dreams had left me emotionally drained, yet a quiet determination simmered beneath the surface. The morning felt heavy, my limbs weighed down by the specters of the night.

Despite the fatigue, a sense of purpose guided my actions. I rose from the bed, each step echoing with the residue of dreams fading away. The coffee shop, a comforting haven where the aroma of freshly ground beans mingled with the hustle and bustle of daily life, called out to me. I was desperate for something normal, something undeniably mortal.

I checked my phone and saw a message from Thalia, as well as the Etsy orders I had yet to start.

Elders accepted my request. I'll reach out if I learn anything. xx

With Thalia following a lead, I felt like I could really focus on and finish the orders I had been putting off. I threw on a sweater and jeans, and grabbed my coat as I was leaving. I took the stairs two at a time and hurried to my moped. Something was calling me to 'Divine Bliss' and I drove as fast as I could.

The wind tousled my hair as I navigated through the winding roads, the promise of a pick-me-up from my favorite café fueling my journey. The familiar landmarks passed by, each turn bringing me closer to my destination. The aroma of freshly ground coffee and the inviting atmosphere of the cafe beckoned from a few blocks away. I could almost taste the rich java as I looked forward to the warm embrace of my favorite drink.

The coffee shop welcomed me with its familiar ambiance. The barista greeted me with a warm smile, a recognition of a regular seeking solace in the midst of the mundane. I ordered my trusty Americano, its warmth promising a much-needed energy boost.

I scanned for an empty seat in the crowded establishment, and grabbed one by the bean counter. In the corner booth the laptop unfolded before me, Etsy orders awaiting attention. The rhythmic tapping of keys provided a soothing cadence. I heard the chime of the bells from the front door, and glanced up out of habit.

"We've got to stop meeting this way," said Adrian Grayson.

He looked amazing, as always. His black fitted mock turtleneck left nothing to the imagination, his six-pack hugged against the unforgiving fabric. His gray pants were much the same, and I ran my eyes from his brown loafers to his waistband. I looked a little lower and my eyes glued to the bulge in his fitted pants. The bulge– so I guess the rumors were true.

"Ah-hem." Adrian coughed.

Shit. Did Adrian Grayson just catch me staring at his dick? I blushed.

"What's your poison?" I asked, trying to ignore the awkwardness I felt with a quick topic change.

He smirked knowingly. "The only thing that gets me through the day is an Americano," he replied. "Iris, right? What is it that you do?"

I nodded. *How do I make my job sound cooler than it is?* I wracked my brain, remembering that Adrian was rumored to be taking over his dad's tech company soon.

"I create specialty, custom, home décor," I told him.

Why do I even care what this rich playboy thinks?

"What do you do?" I pretended I didn't already know. "Are you a tech guy at Vulture?"

"My father owns 'Vulture Network Services' and I report to him," Adrian replied.

"Custom décor, hmm? That's impressive."

I chuckled, a hint of pink tinting my cheeks. "Flattery might just earn you a seat at this table."

As we bantered, the conversation flowed seamlessly, a blend of humor and not so subtle innuendo. Adrian's comments carried a charm that wrapped around me like an enchantment.

He leaned in, his words a murmured invitation. "Iris, I can't help but wonder if your magic extends beyond the realm of interior design."

My heart thudded at the phrasing of his words. "Ma—magic? No magic here," I choked out. "Are you suggesting I have hidden talents, Adrian?"

He grabbed a chair next to me, and a smirk played on his lips. "Perhaps. There's a certain magic in the air when you're around. Or maybe it's just the aroma of your Americano."

I allowed myself to relax. *He clearly throws around the word 'magic' like candy at a parade,* I convinced myself.

I looked at the time on my laptop and my heart dropped. *6:50? How did the time go so fast?*

"So, Iris–"

"I'm late!" I blurted.

"I'm sorry?" Adrian sputtered. He looked like he was not used to being interrupted, and a small part of me felt a little satisfaction.

"I didn't realize how late it had gotten," I apologized. "I have an... appointment at 7:30 that I can't miss."

Why didn't I tell him I have a date?

I quickly packed up my laptop and stood to leave. "Have a good evening, Adrian. Maybe we'll see eachother again," I added as I hurried to the door.

"Iris?"

"Yes?"

"Can I get your last name?"

I smiled slightly. "My name is Iris Kane," I replied. I didn't have time to reflect on Adrian's bewildered expression before I was already out the door.

TEN

The wind rushed past as I zipped through the streets on my ancient moped, the familiar thrum beneath me providing a soundtrack to my thoughts. The sun dipped below the horizon, casting the sky in hues of purple and orange, a calming backdrop to the anticipation building within me. Isaac's invitation echoed in my mind as I maneuvered through the winding roads back to my apartment.

My heart quickened with every passing mile; excitement tinged with a touch of nerves. I parked my moped, and the reality of the evening ahead set in. I rushed inside, the thud of my boots against the floor echoing my haste. The clock on the wall seemed to tick with a knowing rhythm, urging me to prepare for the night.

Isaac's magnetic charm was undeniable, and the

thought of our impending date stirred a flutter in my chest. But, amid the thrill, my mind wandered to the unexpected connection I seemed to share with Adrian Grayson. The ease of our conversation, the playful banter — it lingered in my thoughts like an enchanting spell.

I shook my head, trying to dispel the lingering traces of Adrian's presence. It was a mere coincidence, I reasoned, an unexpected encounter in the coffee shop. Yet, the memory of his deep brown eyes and the magnetic pull between us tugged at my consciousness.

A pang of embarrassment settled in as I rifled through my wardrobe, searching for the perfect outfit. Here I was, contemplating the enigmatic Adrian, while preparing for a date with Isaac. The dichotomy of attraction left me feeling a bit foolish, as if I were juggling the mysteries of my heart.

I settled on a simple yet elegant dress, the plum fabric cascading around me. The reflection in the mirror revealed a mix of anticipation and self-consciousness in my blue eyes. As I applied a touch of makeup, my mind flitted between the two men — one with the allure of mystery, the other with an undeniable magnetism. Isaac's invitation echoed once more, grounding me in the present. I took a deep breath, pushing aside the traces of embarrassment. Tonight was about exploring the connection with Isaac.

I looked down at my watch. *Exactly 7:30, not bad*,
I breathed a sigh of relief. *Something tells me that Isaac
is very punctual.*

As I opened the door, there stood Isaac Thorne,
his charismatic smile momentarily faltering at my
slight tardiness. The bouquet of hyacinths in his hands
exuded a sweet fragrance that filled the air. A subtle
tension hung between us, but Isaac, ever the charmer,
quickly brushed it aside.

"Good evening, Iris. You look stunning," he
complimented, his words a velvet melody that tried to
mend the delicate crack in the evening's ambiance.

I accepted the flowers with a grateful smile, though
I couldn't help but notice the way his gaze lingered on
me. It wasn't the appreciation; rather, it held an intensity that made me feel like a subject under scrutiny,
almost as if he regarded me as a delectable dish to be
savored.

Suppressing the unease that fluttered within, I
chose to ignore it, attributing it to the quirks of my
imagination. Isaac, the consummate gentleman,
extended his arm, and we descended into the night.

A shiny black Mercedes awaited us, gleaming
under the streetlights like a polished gem. The gesture
felt grandiose, and a flicker of discomfort grazed the
edges of my consciousness. 'Love-bombing', they

called it — overwhelming displays of affection and attention meant to captivate.

But, I reminded myself, *it's just one date, and perhaps Isaac's intentions are genuine.*

The restaurant he chose was a local gem, exuding an air of sophistication that matched Isaac's polished exterior. The ambiance was intimate, the soft glow of candles casting a romantic hue over our table. As we settled into the plush seats, I couldn't shake the feeling of being caught in a whirlwind of charm and opulence.

Isaac guided me through the menu, his knowledge of the dishes and wines impressive. The conversation flowed, punctuated by laughter and the clinking of cutlery. But beneath the surface, a subtle undercurrent of unease lingered.

As the evening unfolded, Isaac's attempts to charm me intensified. His compliments were extravagant, his gestures ostentatious. I found myself caught in the dance of his charisma, the magnetism of the night gradually overshadowing the reservations that lingered.

I sipped the wine, the rich flavor lingering on my palate as I contemplated the unfolding events. Love-bombing or genuine affection, it was a fine line to tread. But for now, I decided to immerse myself in the moment, to enjoy the date before making any hasty judgments about Isaac Thorne and the charm he wove around us.

———

The evening with Isaac drew to a close, the fine dining experience winding down as we waited for the bill. Despite the charm and opulence surrounding us, I couldn't shake the realization that something vital was missing—a spark that danced between two people who truly connected on an emotional level, as well as the physical.

Maybe he feels the same way.

As we lingered in that contemplative pause, the ambient hum of the restaurant providing a backdrop, a familiar voice cut through the air. Adrian Grayson, accompanied by a sharply dressed man, strolled by our table on their way to their own.

"Enjoy the rest of your evening, Iris," Adrian said quietly in passing, his amber eyes locking onto mine for a brief moment. There was a hint of genuine warmth in his gaze, and a flicker that seemed to betray a subtle disappointment. His associate nodded politely as they continued toward their destination.

"How do you know Adrian Grayson?" Isaac asked me sharply.

"I–I don't really," I answered him. *Why don't I want to tell Isaac more?*

Adrian's unexpected appearance stirred something within me, a contrast to the polished veneer of the evening with Isaac. The casual exchange, the unspoken understanding between us, resonated more deeply than the elaborate gestures that defined the night. Isaac studied me quietly, but didn't say anything else.

As the server approached with the bill, I decided to trust my instincts. Despite the allure of sophistication and charm, I acknowledged that the genuine connection I sought eluded me in Isaac Thorne. With a polite smile, I reached for my purse, ready to conclude the evening.

"You'll never pay when you're with me," Isaac placed his black card on top of the bill. "Shall we continue the night and get dessert and drinks elsewhere?" He gave his signature smile.

"I have a busy day tomorrow," I lied. "Raincheck?"

He looked irritated again. "What's one drink? I promise I'll get you back home at a reasonable time. Just one drink won't hurt you."

This man is clearly not used to being told no, I rolled my eyes internally.

"I'm sorry, Isaac. But I've had such a wonderful night with you, I really would like another date," I lied again.

My attempt at politeness seemed to strike a chord with Isaac. His suave demeanor crumbled, replaced by an unsettling irritation. The atmosphere shifted as he tightened his grip on my arm, a discomforting display of possessiveness that left me on edge.

Before the situation could escalate further, a timely intervention arrived. Adrian Grayson materialized beside our table, a calm authority in his presence. His warm brown eyes, typically enigmatic, held a subtle intensity as he assessed the unfolding scene.

"Is everything all right here?" Adrian inquired, his tone measured but firm.

I glanced at Adrian, grateful for the unexpected rescue. Isaac, now visibly angry, released his grip on my arm but didn't relent in his dissatisfaction. "Mind your own business, Grayson," he snapped.

Adrian's response was a model of composed restraint. "It becomes my business when a lady is uncomfortable."

"Go back to your dinner and leave my date and I alone," Isaac practically hissed out. "You're not wanted or needed here." He gripped my arm again and stood.

Adrian's steady gaze met Isaac's defiant stare, and a charged silence hung between them. The air crackled with tension, and it seemed the two men were engaged in an unspoken battle, each vying for control of the situation.

Isaac, undeterred, took a step closer to Adrian, his voice dripping with arrogance. "You always think you can play the hero, don't you? What's your interest in her, anyway?"

Adrian's copper eyes flickered with a hint of something inscrutable. "I have no interest in playing games, Thorne. But I won't stand by when someone's well-being is at stake."

The confrontation reached a boiling point as Isaac, overcome by anger, made a sudden move. He let go of me and reached out as if to grab Adrian, but the latter, swift and decisive, deftly sidestepped the aggression. In a moment that seemed to unfold in slow motion, Adrian effortlessly disarmed Isaac, pinning him against the wall with an assertive grip.

"Keep your hands to yourself," Adrian's voice was a low warning, cutting through the tension.

Isaac, now physically overpowered, shot a venomous glare at Adrian. "This isn't over, Grayson. And fuck you, *bitch*." He spat at me, then stormed out of the eatery.

Adrian's gaze shifted from Isaac, concern etched across his features. His amber eyes, once locked in a battle of wills, softened as they met mine. The intensity of the previous encounter dissipated, replaced by a genuine worry. "Iris. Are you okay?"

Adrian's expression remained gentle, a warmth in his eyes. "I think it's best if I get you home," Adrian suggested, his concern lingering.

"What about your dinner?" I asked him, my voice still trembling.

Isaac, having retreated from the scene, cast one last lingering glance through the restaurant window filled with resentment before disappearing into the night. The restaurant, now quieter after the tense exchange, resumed its normal rhythm.

"He'll be fine," Adrian nodded to the man still sitting at their table, who lazily waved back; his attention on the waitress he was trying to proposition.

————

Adrian's sleek navy Audi glided through the quiet streets of Silver Grove as I sat in the passenger seat, the subdued hum of the engine providing an oddly comforting soundtrack. The tension that lingered between us was palpable, an unspoken understanding that echoed in the confined space.

As we neared my apartment complex, I couldn't help but feel a twinge of anxiety at the thought of facing Isaac again. Adrian, sensing my unease, turned to me with a furrowed brow.

"What were you doing with a guy like Isaac Thorne, anyways?"

I looked into his eyes and saw only concern. "He's

my neighbor, he just moved in across the hall from me."

"Iris, I know it's none of my business, but Isaac Thorne is dangerous. Are you sure you're safe living so close to him?"

I sighed, grappling with the reality of my situation. "I appreciate your concern, Adrian. I'll figure things out, but I can't let him drive me out of my home. I've dealt with worse."

He gave me a look I couldn't quite discern, but didn't say anything. "I don't want to see you in danger. Let me help you. I can cover the cost of a hotel until you figure things out. It's the least I can do." His offer held out, tempting and thoughtful.

I considered it for a moment, appreciating the genuine concern he exhibited. But a stubborn determination rose within me.

"Thank you, Adrian. I'll be okay. I can't let Isaac push me around," I asserted, my resolve unwavering.

Lost in the depths of Adrian's eyes, I found myself dangerously close to his lips, the magnetic pull between us undeniable. His intoxicating scent enveloped me, making it difficult to resist the urge to lean in further. The air crackled with unspoken desires, and for a fleeting moment, the world outside the car ceased to exist.

Just as the tension reached its peak, Adrian gently

grabbed my phone, breaking the spell. In a swift, protective gesture, he added his contact information. The reality of the situation rushed back, and I couldn't help but appreciate his thoughtfulness.

You shouldn't be thinking about kissing someone new when you just hooked up with someone else, I chastised myself. *Especially since that someone else ended up being such a dick.*

I reluctantly stepped out of the car, the cool night air providing a necessary distance. Adrian's lingering gaze and the electric atmosphere between us lingered even after the car pulled away. As I made my way into the apartment complex, I glanced back to see Adrian waiting until I safely entered, before driving off into the night.

ELEVEN

In the safety of my apartment, I quickly locked the door behind me, ensuring both mortal security and the enchantments my parents had carefully taught me over the years kept my apartment secure. A sense of relief washed over me, knowing that I could take a moment to breathe without the looming presence of Isaac.

My heart still raced from the awkward encounter, and the memory of Isaac's unsettling gaze, and iron grip lingered in my mind. I rolled up my dress sleeve and trembled when I saw the already purple-red bruise in the shape of Isaac's hand.

I need to calm down.

I shakily poured a glass of wine and sent a quick text to Thalia while I waited for the bath to fill. The warm water, scented with lavender, enveloped me like a comforting embrace. I let the soothing atmosphere ease my tension, trying to wash away the remnants of the disastrous date. I closed my eyes, allowing the sound of the vent fan in the background to mingle with the subtle crackling of scented candles nearby.

The flickering candlelight cast a warm glow, creating dancing shadows on the bathroom walls and enhancing the sense of calm enveloping me. As I reclined in the tub, I became aware of the delicate touch of the water, which seemed to carry away not only the physical dirt but also the emotional residue of the unpleasant evening. I let my mind wander, detaching from the memories of the disastrous date, and focused on the present moment of relaxation.

With each breath, I could feel the stress and frustration dissipating, replaced by a growing sense of renewal. I reached for a bath sponge and a bottle of silky-smooth bath gel, creating fragrant bubbles that added an extra layer of luxury to the experience. The bubbles clung to my skin, creating a soft, effervescent layer that added to the overall sensation of indulgence.

Exiting the tub, I wrapped myself in a plush towel, the residual warmth from the bath comforting me as I stepped back into the real world. Renewed and refreshed, I reached for my phone to see if the Werecat had replied.

I'm coming over, it read simply.

ETA?

I heard a bump and a curse outside my door, and my heart raced. "Iris? Are you in there? Why isn't my key working?"

I took a moment to steady my breathing and inched towards the door. I cracked it open wide enough for my friend, and yanked her inside before closing and locking the door once more.

"Ow!" Thalia yelped. "What's with all the cloak and dagger?"

The glow of candlelight cast a warm ambiance in my apartment as I shared the events of the unsettling date with Thalia. I recounted the discomfort of Isaac's intense gaze, the unease that settled over the evening, and the relief I felt when Adrian intervened like an unexpected knight in shining armor.

Thalia listened intently, her feline eyes reflecting concern. "That sounds absolutely terrifying! I'm glad Adrian was there to help. What did he say when he rescued you?"

I swooned a little when I thought of the protection Adrian had shown me against Isaac. I sighed, still processing the strange turn of events. "He didn't say much, just asked if I was okay. But his presence alone was reassuring. It's like he sensed something was off and stepped in without hesitation."

Thalia's expression softened, and she reached out to grasp my hand. "Well, you're safe now, and that's what matters. And hey, I've got some good news for you, to lighten the mood."

A spark of curiosity lit up within me. "Good news? What happened?"

Thalia grinned, her features turned playful. "I found some information in the Clan archives on the grimoire, and guess what? As your magical skills progress, the unidentified language in the grimoire becomes readable. So, the more you learn, the more the secrets of your familial magic will be revealed."

"That is good news! But what about your necklace?" I asked.

She tugged at the chain and grimaced. "Not as much as I would have liked. All I could gather was that it's enchanted, and it's some sort of conduit. For what, I have no idea. But I'm really banking on that grimoire now to fill in the gaps."

"Well, I'll keep looking! If it's in there, it will all be revealed sooner or later."

In an attempt to shake off the lingering discomfort from the failed date with Isaac, Thalia and I opted for the classic remedy of trashy reality shows. We surrendered ourselves to the mindless drama unfolding on the screen, losing track of time as the night wore on. Despite the distractions, the unsent text to Adrian lingered in the back of my mind. I mulled over the words, questioning whether I should reach out or let the night pass in silence.

The indecision weighed on me, but for now, I chose to keep my thoughts to myself. As the reality shows faded into the background, exhaustion crept in, and the warmth of Thalia's feline form at my feet provided an unexpected comfort. We fell asleep on the couch, surrounded by the soft glow of the TV, dreams of the upcoming ball and the mysteries of the grimoire dancing in my mind.

———

In the passing days leading up to the ball, the anticipation in the air became palpable. Thalia, splitting her time between assisting her mom and the event planner in the intricate preparations, working, and training with the Clan, always found moments to guide me through the labyrinth of spellcasting.

But slowly I was getting better, and more confident. With each passing day, the grimoire became less of an enigma, and the foreign language of magic began to reveal itself to me and flow more naturally from my lips. Thalia's encouragement, and my efforts, were starting to pay off.

The intermediate spells, once daunting, now felt

like familiar companions. Sparks of energy danced in the air as I successfully conjured protective barriers and summoned basic elemental forces. We still hadn't learned anything about Thalia's necklace, but the book was thick.

I didn't feel comfortable practicing new magic in my apartment, and I had even started keeping the Grimoire at Thalia's place. Isaac hadn't made an appearance since that awful night, but I could feel his presence ever-looming, like a black cloud.

I wiped the sweat from my brow and sat down, reaching for my phone.

Hey.

I pressed send on my message to Adrian before I could talk myself out of it. A minute later, my phone buzzed with a reply.

Who is this?

I grit my teeth in embarrassment.

Iris Kane.

Sorry.

I waited while the text bubble blinked, bobbing a leg anxiously.

To what do I owe the pleasure?

I hesitated, and bit my lip.

Just wanted to say thank you for the other night.

I put my phone on silent, leaving it on the couch and walked to the kitchen to search for a bite to eat.

Adrian Grayson, with his enigmatic presence and chiseled features, had become a constant in the recesses of my thoughts.

His cold yet magnetic demeanor, the way his russet eyes bore into mine during our brief encounters, had ignited a spark within me that refused to be extinguished. The magnetic pull, a force I tried to dismiss, lingered, leaving me in a state of heightened awareness whenever his name was uttered.

Thalia sensed the subtle shift in my demeanor. As we practiced spells and discussed the upcoming ball, there were moments when her perceptive gaze lingered a beat too long, studying my heartbeat and subtle glances to my phone. A knowing smile played on her lips, and her feline eyes held a glint of mischief that betrayed her insight into the romantic turbulence that swirled within me.

After our final lesson of the day, I allowed myself to look at my phone. 1 new message from Adrian.

I'm beginning to feel like your knight in shining armor, Iris.

"Who has you grinning at your phone like that?" Thalia asked me.

"I– uh– I–" I stuttered and blushed. "After Adrian saved me that night with Isaac, we've been texting a little." I shrugged, and tried to appear nonchalant.

"Why didn't you say anything?" Thalia exclaimed.

" If this man is making you smile even through text, he must be important."

I tried to shrug again, but gave up halfway through. I should have known better than to hide anything from a Werecat, especially a Werecat that was like a sister.

"So when are you going on a real date with him?"

"I don't think he's interested in me that way. He's the playboy son of a CEO. I sell decór on my Etsy shop. What would he want with me?" I dismissed her words.

A pillow smacked me in the face, and I looked up in shock.

"Don't dismiss yourself like that, Iris! You're a capable, smart, and beautiful woman that anyone would be lucky to earn even one date with. Give yourself more credit!" Thalia's hands rested on her hips, and her eyes glowed with emotion.

"Thanks, kitty cat. You keep me sane," I smiled softly. "Only one more sleep until the ball tomorrow," my eyebrows wiggled playfully. "Let's forget about Adrian for now and focus on that! Are you ready to dance the night away?" I giggled.

"Iris," she said, her voice tinged with a hint of apprehension. "I can't shake this fear that tomorrow might not bring what I've always hoped for. What if I don't find my fated, and my parents are forced to arrange a marriage of alliance?"

Her words hung in the air, a quiet admission of the weight that rested on her heart. I looked at her, searching for the right words to offer comfort. "Thalia," I asked gently, "do you even want to find your fated? Or are you upset about the conditions required for you to rule a Clan?"

Tears welled in her eyes as she nodded, the vulnerability she rarely revealed exposed in that moment. "I do want to find him, Iris. More than anything. It's not just about tradition or the expectations and rules of our society. Even though I enjoy the playful banter, and the sexual connections with other Occults, there's always been a part of me that yearned for something deeper, Werecat or not."

I reached out, placing a comforting hand on Thalia's shoulder. "You're not alone in this, Thalia. Tomorrow is a night of possibilities, and who knows what the magic of the ball might unfold. Fated or not, you deserve a love that's true and genuine."

Thalia nodded, wiping away a tear with the back of her hand. "What about you? Do you want a fated mate, a one true love?"

I nodded slowly. "Though unlikely, I've always wanted to find that special connection, someone who understands the magic within me and complements it with their own. Despite the laughter and the fun, there's a part of me that has been waiting for that elusive dance where our destinies align."

TWELVE

Before the sun had fully embraced the sky, Thalia's mom, Jen, burst into our rooms with a contagious enthusiasm that was impossible to resist. "Wake up, my darlings! It's time to seize the day," she declared, the excitement in her voice propelling us out of bed.

In no time, Thalia and I found ourselves immersed in a whirlwind of preparations, surrounded by an array of decorations that sparkled with celestial charm. Jen, with her boundless energy, orchestrated the setup with a precision that left us in awe. The air buzzed with the scent of fresh flowers and the soft glow of fairy lights that would soon transform the ballroom into a moonlit haven.

Thalia and I worked side by side, weaving strands of ivy and arranging delicate crystals with a shared purpose. The laughter and camaraderie flowed freely, creating an atmosphere that mirrored the magic I helped conjure for the night ahead. As we draped velvet curtains and I placed small glowing orbs of light, the enchantment of the ballroom began to take shape.

Jen, in between bursts of creativity and heartfelt laughter, shared anecdotes from past balls, weaving tales of love and surprises that had unfolded within the very walls we adorned. "I met your father at one of these many years ago, you know," Jen spoke to Thalia with a faraway look in her eyes. "We had known each other for years, but when we locked eyes that night, we were fated."

"Don't get all mushy on me mom," Thalia groaned. "We've heard this story a million times."

I chuckled softly at mother and daughter, and it made my heart ache for my own mom. Jen and Vallin took me in all those years ago, and graciously treated me as their own daughter, alongside Thalia and Ewan. Even the FrostFelt Clan considered me one of their own, which was almost unheard of; Werecats were not the trusting type.

But no matter how much affection and care I was shown, nothing could ever compare to the love I felt from my biological parents. That Occult bastard took them away from me in an afternoon, and disappeared without a trace. My heart twisted at the painful memory, and I didn't realize that I had been crying until Jen put her arm around me.

"We miss them too," she said. "Thalia told me about the grimoire. They would be proud knowing you're continuing their legacy."

I wiped my tears on my sleeve and smiled at the Clan Mother. "Thank you, Jen," I sniffled and hugged her tight.

———

As the morning unfolded into afternoon, and the ballroom transformed into a scene of enchanting beauty, I couldn't help but marvel at the seamless fusion of magic and camaraderie.The scent of fresh Bromeliad blooms, and the hum of activity lingered in the air as the final touches were put in place.

Jen, beaming with pride, declared a brief respite for lunch. I grabbed my phone from my purse nearby, and checked my messages.

It's Saturday, the message from Adrian began. *No need for a hero tonight?*

I couldn't help but roll my eyes. *Are you applying for the job?*

The typing bubble taunted me.

Does it require an interview? He replied.

Of course. How else could I properly vet you? I'm

searching for my knight in shining armor - I don't want to accidentally get another loser in tin foil.

I waited a few minutes, but no text or typing bubble appeared. I sighed and shoved my phone back in my purse.

Sunlight bathed the adorned ballroom, and Jen's discerning eyes swept over the venue with a satisfied smile. "Well done, girls," she praised, her gaze filled with pride. "Go, get yourselves ready for the ball. I still need to confirm a few last-minute details with the chef."

We walked back to Thalia's house, the Werecat excitedly talking the entire way. I listened politely, but my mind was elsewhere.

Why can't I get him out of my head?

My fingers twitched and I mustered my willpower to not check my phone. We walked up to the spacious family home and made our way to our respective quarters, anticipation buzzing like a spell in the air. I chanted a teleportation spell, and my gown and makeup appeared on the bed of the guest room.

As I carefully transferred my phone from my everyday purse to the delicate clutch that matched my gown, a buzz echoed through the room. My heart skipped a beat as I glanced at the screen, discovering a text from Adrian.

How about an interview over dinner? Tonight at 6?

My heart raced. The butterflies in my stomach I had tried so desperately to tame were now feral, threatening to escape.

I can't tonight, my mood soured as I typed. *I have a family thing. How about you bring your resumé to our favorite coffee shop tomorrow morning for brunch? 10ish?*

It's a date, he replied.

I threw my phone on the bed and let myself squeal.

"What's with all the screeching?" Thalia pushed open the door with her manicured foot, both hands trying to put in a stubborn earring. She looked absolutely stunning in her ball gown, the deep black fabric accentuating the feline grace in her movements.

"I think I've got a date tomorrow," my skin turned pink. "With Adrian."

"Well, well, well," she teased, giving me a knowing look. "I fucking knew it! Now, come on. The ball awaits, and we can't keep our admirers waiting."

I took one last look in the mirror on our way out. My kohl rimmed eyes stared back at me, the icy blue glinting with a mix of determination and uncertainty. The dim light in the room cast shadows that danced across my face, emphasizing the high cheekbones and the subtle curve of my lips. I ran my fingers through my tousled, chestnut hair, trying to tame the rebellious strands that insisted on falling across my forehead.

The dress fabric clung to my form, accentuating curves that were usually hidden beneath loose clothing. The gown flowed elegantly as I moved, creating a trail that whispered against the floor with each step. I couldn't help but marvel at the transformation. The lanky figure I was accustomed to, had taken on an unexpected grace.

The gown, once a mere piece of clothing, now felt like a second skin, a manifestation of a different side of me. The navy hue of the dress complemented the cool tones of my eyes, creating a captivating contrast that drew attention to the intricate details of the embroidered stars. Each tiny celestial symbol seemed to tell a story, a constellation of moments woven into the fabric. As the dim light caught the delicate stitches, the stars twinkled, casting a subtle glow around me.

I heard a low whistle and looked into the yellow eyes of Ewan. "Wow, Iris." He said. "You look like an embodiment of the night itself."

I felt a blush rise to my cheeks, a mixture of gratitude and the fluttering excitement that Ewan's words stirred within me. "Thank you, Ewan," I replied, my voice a soft murmur.

———

As we made our way to the grand ballroom, the anticipation in the air was palpable. The melodies of a live orchestra wafted through the air, beckoning us into a world of magic and romance. Thalia linked her arm with mine, and together, we stepped into the elegantly adorned hall, ready to embrace the enchantment of the night.

The ballroom was a vision of beauty, bathed in the soft glow of fairy lights and adorned with ethereal decorations. Couples already twirled gracefully on the dance floor, their gowns and suits a reflection of the night. The air hummed with laughter, lively conversations, and the occasional gasp of delight.

My eyes widened at the wide array of Occult, the most I had ever seen in one place. A range of shifters in various stages of transformation, a smattering of alluring nymphs with their gowns of silken petals, witches and wizards surrounded by the glow of the enchantments they cast as party tricks. My eyes widened when I saw the Veela, their golden hair and pearly skin luminescent in the moonlight.

"Don't stare," Thalia quietly cautioned me. "I know a lot of this is new to you since you didn't have your parents to integrate you into Occult society. But our promise by opening up the guest list this year was that everyone should come as they are and fear no judgment."

I nodded. My cheeks turned pink.

"Especially the Veela," she added. "They don't take kindly to perceived slights." Thalia squeezed my hand kindly. "Just be glad there are no Vampires here, they definitely would have noticed your staring."

I smiled at my friend, determined to enjoy myself tonight. Thalia and I joined the festivities, losing ourselves in the rhythmic swirl of the music. As we danced, my gaze occasionally wandered to the entrance, half-expecting to see a familiar figure. Adrian's message pressed in the back of my mind, and the butterflies in my stomach fluttered with each step I took.

THIRTEEN

As the night unfolded, I found myself caught in a whirlwind of enchantment, the magic of the ball casting its spell on everyone in attendance. Thalia and I danced with fellow Occults, sharing laughter and stories. The atmosphere was electric, with the promise of unexpected connections. As a slow, romantic melody filled the ballroom, Thalia nudged me with a sly grin.

"Open yourself to something new," she said as I was gently pushed towards a Werecoyote that had been eyeing me for the past hour.

"Could I have this dance?" He extended a hand.

I smiled softly and nodded. He was cute, dressed sharply in an all black fitted tux. His curly dark hair bounced loosely over his mesmerizing green eyes. "I'm Trion Whitefang, of the Crimson Hunter Werecoyote pack out in Stormvalley." He gently put his hands around my waist.

"Oh, that's a few hours from here! I'm Iris Kane. Witch, and honorary member of the Frostfelt Clan." My hands rested delicately on his shoulders, and we swayed to the music as we chatted. He was easy to talk to, and I could feel Thalia's approving gaze on us. But he wasn't what I was looking for. And he definitely wasn't Adrian.

Why am I like this? I chastised myself. *You don't know anything about Adrian. For all you know, brunch tomorrow is just a kindness and not a date. Focus on the now, and forget about Adrian Grayson.*

The song ended, and I politely excused myself from Trion. "Thank you for the lovely dance," I said and gave him a genuine smile. He bowed, before disappearing into the crowd.

"No spark?" Thalia asked.

I shook my head. "But I hope he finds his fated tonight, he seems like such a genuine guy."

"Well the night is young, so the odds aren't too bad!" Thalia twirled, the gems on her dress catching in the starlight through the skylight in the ceiling. "I see a Satyr giving me a 'come-hither' look, and who am I to fight it!" She winked at me and sauntered over to the eye-catching half-goat, half-man.

The rhythmic pulse of music wrapped around me

like a cocoon as I watched Thalia twirl through the crowd of Occult, each partner a fleeting shadow in her dance. She looked happy, her laughter mingling with the notes in the air.

But I could sense the undercurrent of something more profound, a subtle ache in her eyes each time a new partner took her hand. It wasn't just a desire for company; it was a longing for a connection with her fated that eluded her with every turn.

The grandeur of the ballroom enveloped me, its opulence and splendor reflected in the shimmering gowns and polished suits that twirled and glided across the dance floor. My eyes involuntarily sought out Ewan, and as I observed from across the room, a pang of mixed emotions coursed through me.

There, amidst the elegant dance, Ewan spun a beautiful Werecat from another Clan. Their movements were harmonious, a symphony of grace and allure that drew the eyes of onlookers. A sense of disappointment lingered within me, a twinge of regret for never seizing the opportunity to share such moments with him.

Perhaps it was the enchantment of the ball, or the ethereal ambiance that enveloped us, but a flicker of determination sparked within. I decided that maybe, just maybe, I could muster the courage to approach him and ask for a dance. As I took a step forward, eager to bridge the distance that separated us, I stopped cold when I felt someone close behind me.

"Iris Kane," a familiar voice said from behind.

I turned, and there he was—Adrian Grayson. His piercing eyes met mine, and a warm smile curved his lips. *Oh goddess, his lips.* "Would you care to join me for a dance?"

The invitation hung in the air, wrapped in the allure of the already magical night. Without a word, I nodded, and he extended his hand, leading me onto the dance floor. He looked amazing, in a bespoke dress shirt and charcoal-colored pants that accentuated his muscular form.

Stop drooling, Iris. Focus on the task at hand. What is Adrian Grayson doing at an Occult-only event?

We swayed together, our movements synchronized with the cosmic rhythm surrounding us. Adrian's hand on mine felt like a bridge connecting two realms, and as we twirled and glided across the floor, whatever was between us grew stronger. His voice, a gentle whisper in the symphony of the night, filled my ears.

"You know, Iris, my family has a long and powerful lineage of Warlocks that spans centuries in Silver Grove," he confessed, his gaze never leaving mine. "When I first heard your name at 'Divine Bliss', it sparked a distant recognition. But when I saw you here, and discovered you were Occult, I was genuinely surprised. A pleasant surprise, I assure you."

I can't believe Adrian Grayson is here.

Our dance continued, a spell weaving around us as if time itself slowed to a waltz. Adrian's touch was both grounding and intoxicating, and I couldn't help but be drawn deeper into the magic that surrounded us. As the music reached its crescendo, Adrian was reluctantly pulled away; duty calling him to converse with an Ifrit—an alliance crucial to the Grayson family's ventures. He held my gaze, regret flickering in his eyes.

"Forgive me, Iris. Duty calls, but I promise, it won't be long," he said, sincerity echoing in his voice. "Save the next dance for me?" He slowly pressed his lips to my hand, and it felt like a flame erupted where his mouth stamped me.

I nodded. Adrian departed, leaving me amidst the enchantment, the echo of his promise lingering in the air. I watched as he navigated through the crowd, a figure of elegance and power.

As I watched the crowd, a middle-aged witch with a cloak of midnight hues approached me, her eyes gleaming with curiosity. "Hello dear, you look vaguely familiar. I am Elfed Deamonne of the Divine Oak Coven. You are a Witch as well, yes? From which Coven do you hail?" she inquired, her voice a melodic whisper.

I sighed, the weight of my past settling on my shoulders like the heavy cloak the Witch wore. "My name is Iris, though I have no Coven. My parents passed away when I was a young teen, and the FrostFelt Clan took me in as their own."

She nodded, her gaze scrutinizing me. "And your last name, dear?"

"Kane," I replied, expecting nothing more than a polite acknowledgement. But her reaction was far from what I anticipated. Her eyes widened, and a gasp escaped her lips as if she'd uncovered a long-buried secret.

"The Kane family is believed to be extinct, including you," she murmured, her words sending a chill down my spine.

"What do you mean?" I asked, my voice barely a whisper, drowned out by the thumping bass that enveloped the room.

She leaned in, her tone a conspiratorial whisper. "The Witches and Warlocks believed your entire family to be deceased, their legacy buried in the shadows. Including you, Iris Kane. What happened to your family is a terrible tragedy."

A shiver coursed through me.. The Occult community, *my peers*, had thought me dead; a ghost of a family erased by the passage of time. The heaviness of their collective ignorance pressed against my chest, leaving me breathless.

"What does this mean?" I sputtered, my mind racing to grasp the implications of my newfound revelation.

"Dark secrets have a way of entwining themselves with the fabric of reality," the witch explained cryptically. "The past is a labyrinth, and not all its corridors are well-lit. Your parents' killer has never been caught, Iris. This may just be a blessing in disguise."

Thalia continued to dance, blissfully unaware of the shadows closing in around me. I felt the tendrils of a long-buried mystery tightening their grip. "I– I need some air," I choked out as I stumbled through the throngs of mingling Occult to the terrace.

The Witch's words lingered in the recesses of my mind like a haunting melody, each syllable a dark note that resonated with the secrets of my past. In cool night air, the weight of the Occult world pressed upon me, suffocating and dense.

The party's lively echoes reached a fever pitch behind me, a cacophony of laughter and music that threatened to engulf my thoughts. The vibrant celebration, once a source of solace, now felt like a pulsating heartbeat that resonated with an unsettling rhythm.

I couldn't shake the feeling that unseen eyes were

upon me, shadows veiled in the darkness, observing my every move. The moon hung low in the sky, its silvery glow casting an eerie pallor over the courtyard. The party's muffled sounds echoed behind me as I ventured into the labyrinth of shadows that sprawled beyond the festivities.

How could everyone think I had died along with my parents?

I turned the corners of the courtyard, seeking solace in the anonymity of the night. The cobblestone paths seemed to twist and turn, as if they held the secrets of countless generations within their worn grooves. The air was thick with a tension that coiled around me, constricting like a serpent in the grass.

I quickened my pace, the cobblestones beneath my feet echoing my hurried heartbeat. The shadows seemed to dance alongside me, their elusive forms flickering at the edge of my vision.

As I walked, the path ahead seemed to stretch into infinity, the ancient trees that lined the courtyard swayed with a ghostly grace, their branches casting grotesque shadows that seemed to whisper secrets only the night could fathom.

Breathe. You're all worked up because of what that Witch told you. Go back and join Adrian and Thalia. Worrying is for tomorrow.

I retraced my steps toward the heart of the party. My heart fluttered erratically, a sense of unease gripping me with every step. The distant laughter and music from the festivities provided little comfort, the lively sounds now a dissonant melody that clashed with the ominous symphony in my mind.

I yearned for the camaraderie of the crowd, the comforting presence of Thalia and, more than anything, the reassuring heartbeat of Adrian. Adrian's heartbeat echoed in my ears, a distant rhythm that called out to me like a siren's song. The yearning intensified, a magnetic pull drawing me closer to the heart of the celebration. I took a deep breath, attempting to shake off the lingering unease, but the shadows clung to me like a cloak of uncertainty.

As I approached the patio my pace quickened, driven by an inexplicable urgency. The party lights spilled through the archways like golden tendrils, beckoning me back to the safety of their glow. But as I reached for the door, a cold hand seized my wrist, squeezing it with an icy grip that made me cry out in pain.

A sinister silhouette emerged from the shadows, its form elongated and grotesque. Isaac Thorne materialized before me, his eyes gleaming with a malevolence that sent shivers through my core. His fangs elongated, bared in a sinister smile.

"I'm not letting you go this time," he hissed, the words dripping with malice.

Fear constricted my chest, but before I could react, he lunged at me with a speed that defied any mortal capability. Time seemed to slow as the world blurred into a chaotic frenzy of darkness. The night swallowed me whole, and my world went black.

A single thought lingered—an echo in the abyss—I had underestimated the depths of the Occult world, and now, I was lost in its embrace, swallowed by shadows that hungered for the light.

FOURTEEN

Darkness clung to me like a shroud as I gradually surfaced from unconsciousness. My senses slowly returned, but the ominous chill that enveloped me sent a shiver down my spine. My hands and feet bound, a biting ache pulsating through my limbs.

Panic surged as I realized my mouth had been gagged, rendering me mute in the face of the unknown. My body was being dragged unceremoniously by the feet, gravel and dirt scraping against my back. Panic surged anew as I strained to see my captor.

The dragging stopped, and I was dumped near a looming mausoleum. The cold stone pressed against my cheek as I struggled to make sense of my predicament. My attempts to scream would be muffled by the gag, leaving only desperate whimpers that would echo nightmarishly through the graveyard.

As my eyes adjusted to the darkness, the silhouette of Isaac Thorne materialized. He paced near the mausoleum, his figure a haunting specter against the backdrop of ancient graves. With a sinister calmness, he pulled out a phone and dialed a number, the faint glow casting an eerie pallor on his malevolent features.

"I have her," he spoke, his voice a chilling whisper that made me break out in a cold sweat. "No, I wasn't followed," he said with annoyance lacing his voice. "I'm sorry, you're right. That was not an appropriate tone to take with you." Isaac's conversation continued in hushed tones, each word carving a deeper well of dread within me. I strained to catch any clue, any fragment of information that might unveil the dark tapestry surrounding me.

But his words remained elusive, it teased the edges of my understanding. He walked over to me, and I pretended to still be unconscious. "Yeah, the stupid bitch is awake. She thinks she can fool me by keeping her eyes closed." He slammed his boot into my ribs and tears came to my eyes. "We'll see you soon."

The cryptic words hung in the air, and my mind raced with the denseness of their implications. *What twisted game am I ensnared in?*

The graveyard's silence mocked my unspoken

questions, as if the very earth beneath me held secrets too horrifying to fathom.

He circled me, a predatory gleam in his eyes. The cold ground pressed against my bound limbs, and the taste of fear lingered like a bitter aftertaste. My attempts to plead through the gag were met with a derisive smirk, and the weight of his presence pressed upon me like a suffocating fog.

"You really know how to ruin a date, Iris," Isaac sneered, his voice dripping with condescension. "But if not for our night that was cut short, I never would have gotten my confirmation."

Confirmation? My heart pounded in my chest, dread and confusion clouding my thoughts.

Isaac's black eyes bore into mine, his gaze unyielding. "I've been watching you, and that Werecat—well, it sealed the deal. You're the Kane girl, the one that went missing all those years ago."

Dread coiled within me, memories flashing like lightning. *The Kane girl*—the whispered tale of a family taken from this world, a young girl who hadn't escaped the clutches of a monster. Only she *had* escaped. A cruel smile played on his lips, his elongated fangs glinting in the moonlight.

"Why do you want me? Why do you care who I am?" I said between chattering teeth.

Isaac circled me, relishing in the torment etched

across my face. "All will be revealed soon, dear Iris," he purred, seizing me with a cruel grip. "You're coming with me to the Realm of Shadow and Bone. Time for you to witness the true power of the Occult."

He dragged me toward the foreboding mausoleum, its stone walls looming like the gates to a hellish abyss. The air crackled with an otherworldly energy, and I knew that stepping into that building meant crossing a threshold into a realm I would be foolish to hope I'd return from. Isaac, with a sinister grace, approached the mausoleum's entrance. The heavy door, adorned with faded engravings of names long forgotten, creaked open, revealing a yawning darkness within. The scent of must and decay wafted from the shadows, and I didn't know whether to cry or gag.

He pushed me forward and the door groaned shut behind us, sealing us in a cocoon of gloom. We walked to a nondescript crypt, and I wondered If I was about to be left here to die. Isaac's eyes glinted with an unholy fervor, and he produced a wicked-looking blade.

The silver edge gleamed ominously in the dim light as he sliced his palm, the crimson liquid welling up. He approached me, and with a swift, calculated motion, he cut into my palm, the pain merging with a surge of unearthly power.

He saw my eyes widen at the blood in his palm and he smiled sickeningly. "Didn't think Vampires could bleed, hmm? Well, this isn't exactly my blood. It's a cumulation of whomever I ate earlier, as well as my own essence. But still, the magic of the door knows I am who I say I am - an Occult."

The blood, now a macabre blend of life forces, acted as a key. The symbols on the mausoleum walls pulsed with dark magic, and a heavy door before us groaned open, revealing a long, dark corridor that seemed to descend into the very bowels of the earth. The only light emanated from the dim glow of unearthly symbols etched into the stone walls. The corridor stretched endlessly, its length obscured by shadows that seemed to dance and writhe with a malevolent life of their own.

I am so fucked, I thought. *No one saw me leave. I'm going to die here. I can't even attempt any of the spells I've been learning because my mouth is gagged. I'm going to fucking die here.*

Isaac noticed me spiraling and laughed. "Can't give away any more trade secrets I'm afraid. And once again knocked me unconscious.

———

As consciousness clawed its way back into my awareness, I found myself in a disoriented haze, my senses gradually untangling the knots of confusion. The air was thick with the scent of dust and decay, and the cold, unyielding surface beneath me hinted at an unwelcome reality.

I noticed a simple gold bracelet adorning my wrist, and I tried to claw it off to no avail. Slowly, the throne room materialized around me, its opulence serving as a stark contrast to the bruises that adorned my battered body.

Blinking away the remnants of my confusion, I attempted to push myself upright. The effort sent a jolt of pain through my limbs, a reminder of the unnecessary cruelty Isaac had shown me. Amidst the cold stone, a figure materialized. Isaac.

His unimpressed gaze bore into me, the twisted corners of his lips betraying a sadistic satisfaction. His presence exuded a malevolence that seemed to intertwine with the very fabric of the realm.

"So, you've awakened," he drawled, his voice dripping with disdain. "Don't get too comfortable, Iris. This isn't your final destination. I'll be back soon with our queen."

The echo of Isaac's footsteps faded, leaving me in a desolate silence that felt more suffocating than the graveyard's darkness.

His statement hung over me like a dark cloud, and my mind conjured images of a malevolent monarch ruling over this *Realm of Shadows.* The throne itself, a grotesque monument carved from dark stone, loomed over me like a silent judge. Its design spoke of arcane symbolism, the arms adorned with twisted figures that seemed to writhe in perpetual agony. The very air in the room vibrated with an otherworldly power, as if the throne itself held dominion over the shadows.

———

Isaac's footsteps echoed through the desolate corridor, a herald of impending doom. His voice sliced through the stillness, each word a chilling decree. "Welcome to the Court of Shadows, Iris. This is–" he gestured toward the magnificent wooden door, a grotesque smile playing on his lips.

I followed his gaze to the shadows that clung to the walls, an ethereal figure emerging like a specter from the darkness. The queen, a monarch draped in veils of shadow, presided over the chamber with ominous majesty.

I gaped. "Aunt Evelyn?"

FIFTEEN

The realization struck like a bolt of lightning, and my breath caught in my throat. Memories of family photos, glimpses of a face that had been hidden from me for years, surged through my mind. Evelyn, the estranged aunt, a phantom from a past I had only heard whispers of.

I cautiously accepted Evelyn's offered hand, gingerly rising from the cold, unforgiving floor. The apology for Isaac's earlier rudeness hung in the air, a thin veil attempting to mask the deeper complexities of this eerie realm. Evelyn's voice, though composed, carried an undercurrent of calculated grace that hinted at layers of manipulation beneath the surface.

"You are a guest in my realm, Iris, not a prisoner," Evelyn intoned, her words a delicate dance that sought to reassure even as it left questions unanswered. "Isaac can be... intense. I will ensure this won't happen again."

Her cryptic words fueled the unease that had settled in my bones, a gnawing uncertainty about the dynamics at play in this shadowed kingdom. Yet, as she led me through the corridors of the hauntingly beautiful castle, I found myself momentarily captivated by the opulence that surrounded us.

The tapestries, woven with threads of rich hues, depicted scenes both enchanting and foreboding. Plush furniture adorned with intricate carvings offered a stark contrast to the austere throne room. This castle was a paradox, a symphony of elegance and darkness that resonated with an unsettling harmony.

We walked up two flights of stone steps and stood outside of a nondescript wooden door. She acknowledged the bruises that adorned my body, her words carrying a fleeting hint of genuine concern. "Let's get you cleaned up," she promised, and gestured to what I had thought was an empty hallway, bar us. Two stunning dark elves stepped out of the shadows, and I jumped.

"These handmaids will tend to you, Iris." Evelyn informed me. The elves bowed to her and then me, and I nodded back to them a little uncomfortably.

"Get cleaned up and rest, and you can join me for dinner in the evening." Evelyn patted me on the shoulder gently, before striding down the hall.

"Wait!" I called out. "Do you know where this bracelet came from?" I help up my wrist with the delicate gold chain.

"Simply so we don't lose track of you, my precious niece! See you soon," she said, and walked away.

I watched her go, thinking about her words. I turned to the handmaids. "I'm Iris," I said shyly.

One of the handmaids pushed open the door to my room, then turned to look at me. "I am Rani," she said. "This is my sister, Karzhi."

Standing tall and regal, their almond-shaped golden eyes sparkled. Cascading down their slender shoulders, their lustrous black hair shimmered, one in loose braids and one in a tight bun, which was a radiant contrast to the rich hues of their emerald-green dresses.

While the sisters shared the same delicate, pointed ears and graceful features that defined their elven heritage, subtle differences set them apart. Karzhi's gaze held a quiet wisdom, an ancient knowing that seemed to echo through the ages, while Rani's eyes sparkled with juvenile curiosity.

As I stepped through the wooden door, I was greeted by a room of sumptuous extravagance. The towering vaulted ceiling, adorned with intricate golden filigree, imparted a sense of majesty to the room. Cascading from the ceiling, lavish drapes in deep, purple hues framed the tall windows, allowing filtered sunlight to dance across the room. The windows themselves were crowned with stained glass depicting scenes of mythical tales, casting a kaleidoscope of colors upon the polished marble floor.

Against the far wall, a massive four-poster bed stood as the focal point, draped in silken canopies that billowed like clouds caught in a gentle breeze. The bed's intricately carved mahogany frame showcased the craftsmanship of skilled artisans, while the bedding itself boasted the finest silks and velvets, adorned with embroidered symbols of ancient nobility.

Every corner of the castle bedroom bespoke luxury and refinement, creating an atmosphere that transported its occupants to a realm of regal indulgence. I raised my eyebrows, impressed.

"Allow us to prepare you for your dinner with her majesty," Rani said.

I nodded, still dazed from everything that had happened in the past 24 hours. With a courteous bow, they approached me, their movements synchronized in a dance of unspoken harmony. Kharzi drew a bath that looked like liquid moonlight, the water imbued with a gentle warmth and essential oils that promised relaxation.

As I submerged into the fragrant embrace, the worries of the past hours melted away, and everything that had happened so far seemed like a distant dream.

The touch of their hands was gentle yet purposeful as they cleansed away the traces of struggle and dust, revealing the mostly unblemished canvas beneath. Layers of grime dissipated in the water, leaving me feeling reborn. Karzhi clicked her tongue at my bruises, but otherwise didn't remark.

After the bath, they wrapped me in the softest towels, as if swathing me in the embrace of a cloud. Dressed in a gown of blood red velvet, the fabric trailing behind me like a descent of shadows, I couldn't help but marvel at the quality. The gown, adorned with subtle silver embroidery, accentuated the regal ambiance of the room.

As they worked on my hair, the handmaids transformed my tangled brown locks into a fountain of waves, interwoven with delicate silver filigree that shimmered like starlight. Their fingers moved with an artistry that spoke of centuries of practice, each strand becoming a testament to their skill.

My makeup was applied with a deft touch, enhancing my features while maintaining an air of natural allure. Their choice of colors mirrored the celestial palette, from the soft blush of dawn to the muted hues of twilight.

I attempted a simple incantation I had practiced with Thalia; a small flame to light the candle on the vanity. But nothing happened.

"The bracelet is a power dampener, miss," Rani told me. "Our majesty will remove it when she knows you better." I chose not to remark on the gold band that Rani still wore.

I glanced at my reflection, feeling a twinge of discomfort at the riches and secrets surrounding me. The handmaids, however, regarded their work with satisfaction, and nodded with approval.

Despite the unease of being tended to like royalty, I couldn't deny the undeniable truth – they had succeeded in making me look and feel extraordinary. And perhaps, just for this moment, I could allow myself to revel in the enchantment they wove around me, and push my concerns to the back of my mind.

Time to feel out my long lost aunt. Who also just so happens to be a freaking queen. A lot has changed since those pictures I saw in the photo albums.

The handmaids, ever silent, escorted me down the corridor with a natural grace. As we traversed the ancient passageways, I couldn't help but observe the inhabitants of Evelyn's court as they slunk by.

Members of the court, draped in luxurious attire,

were shrouded in an intriguing dance of shadows. Some had shadows that clung to them like loyal companions, trailing their every step with an almost sentient devotion. Others seemed to wear veils of shadow, obscuring their features and lending an air of mystery to their presence. It was as if darkness itself had chosen each member as its canvas, crafting an artful tapestry of concealment.

We came upon the great hall, with its towering pillars and intricate murals, echoed with hushed conversations that ceased abruptly upon our entrance. Eyes, partially hidden in the penumbra of cloaked figures, followed our progress. I sensed the weight of their scrutiny, each member of Evelyn's court bearing the enigma of their obscured identities.

"Everyone out," Evelyn announced. "I would like to dine with my niece alone."

The great hall emptied with an almost unnatural swiftness, leaving Evelyn and me in a solitude woven with the threads of unspoken secrets. The echoing footsteps faded into the distant recesses of the castle, swallowed by the veiled whispers of shadows.

Seated at the grand table, the air was charged with an eerie quiet, as if the very walls held their breath in anticipation. The flickering torches cast dancing shadows across the expanse of the room, creating an otherworldly ambiance that heightened the mystique of the moment.

Servants, almost imperceptible in their movements, began to bring forth an extravagant feast fit for a queen. The aroma of exotic spices and succulent dishes filled the air, awakening my senses to the sensory symphony unfolding before me.

Evelyn, regal in her poise, gestured gracefully toward the array of culinary delights that adorned the table. "Help yourself," my aunt smiled at me.

As I took in the lavish spread before me, my curiosity mingled with a sense of unease. The servants, draped in obsidian garments, moved silently like specters, their faces veiled by the umbral shroud that concealed their features. I watched as the Shadow Queen took a large bite out of a perfectly cooked turkey leg, and my stomach grumbled.

I scooped buttery mashed potatoes in my mouth and almost moaned with pleasure. I sipped the honey-wine, but it tasted so good that I couldn't help but finish the goblet. I heard my aunt chuckle, and I looked at her, my cheeks turning pink.

"This Realm," Evelyn began, her eyes gleaming with knowledge, "is a realm of power, Iris. Here, the throne is not an inheritance bound by blood; it is a manifestation of dominion over the shadows, a testament to one's command of the arcane."

Well that sort of explains it. I guess I don't hail from a long line of royal Witches.

The very essence of this realm seemed to pulse with an unfamiliar energy, and I swear I felt a tingling awareness of the shadows that enveloped us. When I gathered the courage to inquire about her ascension to the throne, her response was as elusive as the shadows that whispered around us.

A subtle dodging of the question, a dance of words veiled in secrecy. I sensed the evasion but chose not to press, my instincts warning me to tread cautiously in this realm of veiled intentions.

Evelyn's gaze subtly shifted, a calculated inquiry veiled behind the guise of casual conversation. "Tell me, Iris," she said, her voice a melodious cadence, "what became of the family grimoire? A relic of our lineage, lost to the currents of fate."

I hesitated, uncertainty flickering in the depths of my gaze. Trust, a fragile thread in this shadowy tapestry, held me back from revealing the truth. "Wasn't it thought lost?" I replied cryptically. A careful dance of words.

I observed Evelyn keenly, discerning a fleeting hint of frustration that flitted across her expression. "It was indeed," my aunt replied slowly.

"I have a few things to take care of tomorrow, Iris.

Would you care to explore the palace grounds until dinner?"

I nodded, and smiled politely. An opportunity to unravel the mysteries in this enigmatic realm awaited me, and I embraced it with vigorous agreement.

Sixteen

A gentle knock echoed through my room, and as the door creaked open, I found myself face to face with a handsome dark elf with eyes and skin the color of the night sky, dressed in all black leathers. His chiseled features gave nothing away.

"I am your escort for the day," he announced with a courtly bow, his voice resonating with a certain grace that bespoke a familiarity with the shadows. The notion of a chaperone stirred a subtle discontent within me, but I masked it beneath a polite nod. Unspoken reservations lingered, shrouded in the shadows that clung to the walls.

The handmaids silently ushered me into the elaborate ritual of preparation. A cascade of gowns awaited, each more resplendent than the last. Their fingers deftly worked through my hair, weaving it into an intricate braid, and my makeup was subtle today. I submitted to the meticulous care of the handmaids, their touch a dance of shadows and silk.

My silent escort trailed behind me as I ventured through the labyrinthine halls of Evelyn's shadowed realm. An air of quiet intrigue lingered, whispers of concealed conversations and veiled gazes that trailed along unseen paths. The castle's occupants observed me with an intensity that made me want to run back to my room.

We emerged into the courtyard, and a surreal landscape unfolded before my eyes. The flora of the Shadow Realm revealed its dark beauty—flowers adorned with petals that seemed to absorb the very essence of the sunlight. The ethereal glow of luminescent plants cast an otherworldly radiance, transforming the courtyard into a twilight haven.

The silence between the dark elf and I held a certain weight, punctuated only by the rhythmic echo of our footsteps on the shadow-kissed ground. As I wandered, the royal stables emerged from the fog like a hidden gem waiting to be discovered.

Intrigued, I entered the stables and was met with a surprising sight—majestic creatures with wings, unearthly beings waiting to be ridden through the skies. The stable hand slowly approached me, with a knowing gleam in their eyes.

"These creatures," the stable hand began, their voice a whisper in the quietude, "are remnants of ancient alliances between the beings of shadow and those who sought dominion over the night skies. Each has a tale, a history that intertwines with the very fabric of the Shadow Realm."

"Thank you for sharing this with me," I breathed out. My eyes were still focused on a creature that resembled a large horse, but was only made of bones and writhing shadows.

"That's a *Rennik*," the stablehand said. "Beautiful, powerful, and incredibly hard to break. But they bond for life to whoever manages to do so."

I watched as the Rennik pawed at the ground, steam flowing from its bony nostrils. The stablehand turned away to continue caring for the creatures, and I took that as my cue to leave. I walked with purpose back to the warmth of the castle, and pulled off my cloak and gloves once inside.

"I want to learn more about this realm, and the creatures that inhabit it," I turned to my guide. "Where can I find that information?"

"You are not allowed in the royal library," he told me.

"And why is that?" I put my hands on my hips.

But he wouldn't answer, and with a still-gloved hand, gestured in the direction of my room. Reluctantly, I followed the Dark Elf's guidance, my steps echoing in the spacious corridors. Disappointment clung to me as we retraced our steps to the bedchambers assigned to me. Before he could fade into the obscurity of the castle's corridors, I stopped, and summoned the courage to voice my petition.

"Wait," I called, my tone a mix of frustration and curiosity. The Dark Elf turned, their gaze as inscrutable as ever.

"Can't you at least go to the library? Get the books I want?" I questioned, my request tinged with a hint of defiance. With a subtle nod, the dark elf departed, leaving me alone once more.

───────

Evelyn's Palace of Shadows had begun feeling like a gilded cage, each opulent corridor hiding more secrets than it revealed. The allure of exploration tugged at me like a relentless current, urging me to step beyond the confines of my lavish chambers. I prepared to venture out alone.

The Elf is probably still at the library. Now's my chance.

But my quest for autonomy was thwarted by the sudden appearance of the handmaids, their graceful figures seemingly materializing from thin air. They informed me that I couldn't leave without a guard as my chaperone, and ushered me back into my room. The restriction left me with more questions than answers, but I chose to keep my inquiries silent.

As the Dark Elf returned with a handful of books, my suspicions deepened. The conspicuous absence of tomes on the realm's history raised questions.

Why keep such vital knowledge veiled in secrecy? Is Evelyn's Palace of Shadows concealing more than just its name suggested?

"I'll be back to escort you to dinner," the Elf bowed and retreated.

I shut the door and perched on an exquisite chaise in my lavishly appointed room. I opened one of the books at random, and pulled a nearby throw onto my chilly legs. Each page unfolded a tapestry of knowledge about the magical creatures inhabiting the Shadow Realm. The descriptions painted vivid images of ethereal beings, all of their forms bathed in hues of darkness.

As the enchanting narratives transported me into the realm of mystical fauna, a knock echoed through the door, shattering the tranquility of my solitary exploration. The Dark Elf, a silent sentinel, stood ready to escort me to dinner with Evelyn. Closing the book reluctantly, I followed him through the dimly lit corridors, the allure of the mysterious creatures lingering in my thoughts.

He bowed when we reached the great hall, then retreated. Another lavish dinner awaited, a banquet of extravagant dishes adorned the table. The air buzzed with an unspoken tension, a silent undercurrent beneath the façade of regality.

Evelyn's gaze bore into me as she once again broached the subject of the elusive family grimoire. Her inquiries, veiled in sophistication, probed the depths of my knowledge. This time, my response lacked the evasive dance, and I decided she was not to be trusted.

"I have no inkling of the grimoire's whereabouts," I said with saccharine sweetness.

The atmosphere in the grand hall shifted abruptly. Evelyn, her elegant poise momentarily disrupted, rose from her seat with indignation. The shadows seemed to coalesce around her in a dance of disapproval.

"Enough," she declared, her voice cutting through the tension. Instructing the Dark Elf to escort me back to my chambers, she retreated into the recesses of the palace, leaving behind an enigmatic echo of frustration.

SEVENTEEN

Morning light filtered through the luxurious drapes as Evelyn, a portrait of regal poise, graced my chambers. The air, thick with tension, carried the weight of unresolved questions. Evelyn's eyes locked onto mine, and her words cut through the serene façade.

"If honesty eludes you, Iris," she murmured, a subtle threat lingering beneath her calm exterior, "perhaps solitude will guide your reflections."

The vague ultimatum hung in the air. "I won't aid your schemes," I declared, my voice a steady rebuke.

She wouldn't really send her only niece to a dungeon, right?

Evelyn's response was swift and unyielding. A summons echoed through the palace, drawing forth Isaac, whose presence carried an air of cold authority.

As he entered what was once my sanctuary, Evelyn's command was clear—he was to drag me to the dungeons by any means necessary.

Karzhi bumped into me as I staggered to my feet. "Strength endures in the quietest hearts," she whispered to me. I did my best to not draw attention from the now missing bracelet on my naked wrist.

———

The cell's cold walls pressed against me as I staggered into its confines, my limbs still aching from the way Isaac had gripped me, and dragged me down the dungeon stairs. The air within was stale, heavy with the scent of ancient stone and the lingering shadows of forgotten despair. I could hear the wails and moans of pain from other prisoners, but I couldn't see anyone else.

Isaac's presence loomed behind me, a specter of malevolence that seemed to seep into the very walls. With a disdainful gesture, he removed the gag, the sudden freedom to speak doing little to ease the rising tide of dread within me. The metallic taste of blood lingered on my lips, a cruel reminder of the ritual that had opened the passage to this forsaken place.

Isaac's voice sliced through the silence like a chilling wind. "I'll be back soon, Iris."

A promise laced with ominous intent. The cell door creaked shut behind me, its heavy iron bars sealing me within a tomb of shadows.

The cell was a symphony of despair—a lone cot against the cold stone, a flickering lantern casting feeble light, and iron bars that seemed to mock any hope of escape. I pressed my palm against the unforgiving stone, the cool touch a cruel reminder of my imprisonment. Fear coiled within me, its tendrils tightening with every passing moment.

I tried chanting the summoning spell I had become so familiar with, picturing my grimoire in my mind's eye. Nothing. I tried again, expending all of my focus. Nothing. The bracelet was gone, but I still could do no magic. The minutes stretched into an eternity, and each echoing sound seemed to herald Isaac's return.

Every creak and rustle in the shadows amplified my anxiety, as if the essence of the realm conspired to torment me. I yearned for sunlight, the comforting embrace of familiar surroundings, but all that surrounded me was an abyss that swallowed every flicker of hope.

As the lantern's feeble glow danced on the cell walls, I whispered a silent prayer for escape. But the shadows were indifferent, and the cell remained an impenetrable fortress. The air grew thick with the mass of impending doom, and the taste of fear lingered on my tongue like a bitter poison.

The heavy Clank of keys signaled the Vampire's return, and I pressed against the cold cell bars, anxiety tightening my chest. The door swung open with a mournful creak, revealing Isaac's silhouette.

Without a word, he seized me, his grip unyielding as he dragged me from the cell. The cold stones beneath me blurred as I stumbled through the corridor, a helpless pawn in the twisted game orchestrated by someone that was supposed to be family.

"What did I do to deserve this?" I begged Isaac for an answer. But he stayed silent, with only the grip on my arm tightening painfully.

Up an unfamiliar narrow staircase we ascended, Isaac's relentless pull never wavering. The air grew heavier with every step, a tangible tension that hung like a thick veil that choked me.

As we reached the top, the staircase spilled us into an opulent expanse that contrasted starkly with the desolation below. The flickering torches cast dancing shadows that played on the ornate walls, creating an illusion of movement within the stillness.

We reached the throne room, a cavernous expanse hidden within the depths of this realm. The air within was thick with ancient energy, as if the very stones remembered the whispers of forgotten rulers who had once presided over this shadowy domain.

Isaac tossed me into the center of the room, the impact sending a jolt of pain through my already bruised and sore limbs. The oppressive silence was broken only by the soft echoes of Isaac's footsteps as he approached the throne.

———

Her eyes, pools of darkness that seemed to drink in the very essence of my soul, met mine. She descended from the throne, her steps echoing in the silence. Aunt Evelyn now sat before me as a regal specter, her gaze penetrating the barriers of estrangement.

My mind raced to grasp the gravity of the situation. Questions flooded my thoughts—*why had Evelyn severed ties with my mother? Why had I been kept in the dark about my aunts existence?* And most importantly–*what is she going to do to me to get what she wants?*

Evelyn's voice filled the room. "Iris, my blood runs in your veins, a connection you can't escape. I know you found the family grimoire; long thought lost to time and circumstance." She stood in front of me.

"I am a reasonable ruler," she said. "Give me the grimoire. And instead of throwing you back into your cell to rot, you can help me." She played with a loose strand of my hair. "We can chalk all of this up to a silly misunderstanding."

The room seemed to contract around me, and I struggled to breathe. The Queen of Shadows was a tyrant. A maelstrom of emotions churned within me —betrayal, disbelief, and a profound sorrow that cut to the core of my soul.

Steel yourself.

"Why should I help you?" I asked defiantly.

She smiled. "Because if you don't, I'll kill you. Just like I had your parents killed, thirteen years ago."

I sputtered. *She was the one who killed my parents? Her own fucking sister?*

"Why would you kill my parents?" I spoke with a tremble in my voice, though I kept my chin held high.

Her lips curled into another sinister smile, a gesture that sent a chill down my spine. Her gaze met mine, a recognition lingering in the depths of those eyes that had witnessed my struggles from afar.

"You see, Iris," she said, "your parents were obstacles, unwilling to submit to the greater design. They held the grimoire, a key to power beyond their comprehension. Power that they refused to relish in. But when they refused to relinquish it, they sealed their fate."

The truth, as horrific as it was, unfolded before me like a nightmare. My parents, taken from me in a brutal act of betrayal orchestrated by family. Evelyn, the orchestrator of their demise, stood before me like a wicked puppeteer.

Her revelation hung in the air like a poison, seeping into the very core of my being. The Queen of Shadows, my estranged aunt, spoke with a haunting calmness, as if the admission held no weight, no remorse. My parents' murders—a dark tapestry woven by her hands.

A chill gripped my heart, the enormity of the betrayal paralyzing my senses. The grimoire had unknowingly held the key to my family's doom. The day of the murders, my parents, sensing the danger, had spelled it away, hiding it from Evelyn's clutches. They had paid the ultimate price for their defiance.

"I searched for that grimoire for years, Iris," Evelyn continued, her eyes gleaming with an unholy fervor. "Your parents' final enchantments made it, and you, elusive, but the moment you found it, the ancient spells reactivated. The threads of destiny wove you into the pattern."

The room seemed to close in, shadows converging around me. "What do you want with the grimoire?" The question escaped my lips, a fragile plea for under-standing.

"Power, Iris," she whispered, her voice dripping with a venomous clarity. "The grimoire holds the secrets to ancient magic, ready to be unlocked. Long ago we ruled the mortal realm. Thanks to my magic, and the grimoire, Occults will rule it once again. Your parents were fools to deny me. Will you make the same mistake?"

She ran a manicured finger along my cheek, and I tried not to show my disgust. "Consider the power that awaits you. The grimoire can unlock realms of magic beyond your wildest dreams. Why resist the destiny that calls for you?"

Don't help this tyrant, no matter what she does or says.

"I won't be part of your fucked up plans, Evelyn. I will never be a pawn in your games."

Evelyn's eyes flickered with a dangerous glint, and the calm façade fractured, revealing the storm beneath. Anger, a tempest that had been brewing for years, surged to the surface. "You underestimate the price of defiance, Iris. The dungeons hold secrets even *you* can't fathom."

The threat hung in the air, a tangible menace that wrapped around me like shackles. The dungeons—the prospect of that dark abyss loomed like a guillotine over my defiance. Fear whispered at the edges of my courage, but I steeled myself against the encroaching dread.

She killed your parents, I reminded myself.

"Or perhaps," Evelyn's voice dropped to a venomous whisper, "I should grant Isaac free reign. Let him extract the location of the grimoire from you, with methods he deems fit."

The mere mention of Isaac's sadistic hands reaching into the depths of my vulnerability sent shivers through my core. I couldn't allow myself to break, to become a vessel for their insidious desires.

I spat at Evelyn's feet, a defiant act that unleashed the rage within her. The room pulsed with energy as she recoiled. Stripped of her veneer, the Queen of Shadows glared at me with fury.

"You little fucking bitch," she hissed at me.

"Isaac!" She barked, and he quickly appeared with a sharp, curved, knife.

"I'm a little old fashioned when it comes to giving pain," the Shadow Queen smiled. "The price of disobedience may be more than you can bear."

Fuck.

I skittered back from her, my limbs tangling up in each other. She watched me with amusement, the thick, short knife gripped in a gloved hand.

I couldn't seem to find my footing fast enough to stand, but it didn't matter. I had backed up as far as I could go, my shoulder blades bumping against some-one's legs. I looked behind me and my breath hitched. Isaac.

"Now, now, pet," Evelyn gestured to the Vampire, who used a foot to kick me towards the queen. I winced, but refused to give him the satisfaction of him hearing me cry out in pain.

"This is just a taste of what will come if you don't get the grimoire to me," she grabbed my chin and tilted it upwards to expose my neck.

I swallowed, and my estranged aunt smiled as my throat bobbed. She pressed the cold metal to my right clavicle and sliced downwards, stopping directly above my left breast. I couldn't hold in the sounds of my pain this time, and a pitiful whine escaped. Blood trickled from the incision she made, and Evelyn stepped back to admire her handiwork.

"That won't kill you, but infection can easily take over in a dirty place, like the cell you can now call your home. Summon the grimoire and I will heal you, wipe your memory, and send you back to the mortal realm like nothing ever happened."

Don't let your parents death's be for nothing.

"Fuck. You." I said. I ripped a piece of fabric from the bottom of my dress and tried to dab at the wound on my chest.

"Very well," Evelyn replied, and gestured to Isaac. "Take her back to her cell and let her rot until I say differently. No food, water only."

———

The cell welcomed me back with its cold embrace, the air heavy with the failures a rebellion cut short. My limbs ached, the remnants of Evelyn's wrath still lingering on my bruised and bloody skin. The cell's confines seemed to constrict around me, a spectral prison that held me captive in the heart of shadows.

Isaac stood beyond the bars, his figure casting an elongated shadow on the damp stone walls. His gaze bore into mine, a cruel reminder of the malevolence that lurked within the Occult's realm. He spoke with a cold detachment that sent shivers down my spine.

"You've made a grave mistake, Iris," Isaac sneered, his voice a sinister whisper that echoed in the confines of the cell. "Evelyn won't be as forgiving the next time."

That was her being forgiving? I shivered.

Isaac leaned against the cell bars, his onyx eyes locking onto mine. "You need to summon the grimoire, Iris. There's no escaping it. Whether you do it willingly or not, we *will* have our way."

A bitter taste of dread coated my words as I replied. "I already tried, when you first threw me in this goddess forsaken place. My magic, it's not strong enough. I can't summon the grimoire even if I wanted to help you. Which I don't."

Isaac's cold laughter filled the cell, a haunting

sound that reverberated against the stone walls. "In each cell, magic is nullified, Iris. The black salt ensures that even the most potent Occult powers are rendered useless. You can't escape, and you can't resist." He casually pushed away from the cell bars.

"And trust me, Iris, whether you help willingly or not, I don't care. The outcome will be the same, if it's up to me."

The echoes of Isaac's departure waited in the cold air, leaving me alone in the oppressive silence of the cell. Curling up on the cell cot, I felt the tremors of fear coursing through my veins. The weight of my powerlessness within these walls pressed upon me, amplifying the isolation that echoed in the cavernous silence. My breaths came in shallow gasps as I grappled with the reality of my predicament.

Panic clawed at the edges of my consciousness. The cell seemed to close in around me as I contemplated the two stark choices that loomed before me. "I'm either going to die alone in this hellhole," I whispered to the shadows, my words swallowed by the crushing stillness. "Or I'll eventually succumb to Evelyn's demands. Maybe both."

The cell walls absorbed my words, offering no solace or reprieve. The thought of succumbing to Evelyn's whims infuriated me, the image of her cruel smile etched in my mind. The prospect of enduring her torture methods filled me with a dread that eclipsed the confines of the cell.

———

I awoke to the unsettling gaze of Isaac, his eyes bearing into my vulnerability like shards of glass. The dim light in the cell flickered, casting dancing shadows that seemed to mock my helplessness. Disgust crawled beneath my skin, as I realized his watchful eyes had been on me, even in the vulnerability of sleep.

The Vampire's twisted sense of amusement manifested as he kicked a bottle of water towards me. It rolled across the damp floor, a cruel invitation that did little to quench the thirst that gnawed at my throat. The sound of my grumbling stomach echoed in the cell, a mockery of my desperate circumstances.

A hollow laugh escaped Isaac's lips as he observed my discomfort. "Hungry, Iris? Thirsty? Helping Evelyn could make all this go away. But she grows impatient, and I can't promise her offer will last much longer."

Despite my hunger and fear, I scoffed at the vampire. "Her offer? To wipe my memories of this and send me on my way after I've betrayed all mortals? How *very* fucking generous." I rolled my eyes and he hissed.

I met his gaze with defiance, my voice a whisper that echoed in the silence. "I will *never* help you."

Isaac's patience, thin as a wisp of smoke, evaporated in an instant. He moved with predatory grace, his fingers curling around the cell bars. The metallic groan of the door opening sent a shiver down my spine. The darkness beyond the cell door seemed to extend infinitely, an abyss that threatened to consume me.

As the door swung open, Isaac's figure loomed in the threshold—a harbinger of pain and torment. The shadows clung to him like loyal attendants, amplifying the malevolence that radiated from his very being.

"You really are a stupid bitch," Isaac growled, his voice dripping with malice. "Allow me to teach you the consequences of defiance."

The cell door closed behind him, sealing me within the darkness once more. Dread settled like a heavy cloak, and I scrambled to the corner farthest from him, Curling in a ball to make myself as small as possible.

Nowhere to hide. Don't let Isaac see your fear.

He stalked towards me and gave me another one of his signature smiles, before grabbing my left hand. "A finger for each insult you've spat at me today," as he quickly bent back the pinky and ring finger until I heard two sickening snaps. I shrieked.

"Please," I begged. "Just let me go."

"Are you ready to summon the grimoire now?" He ignored my request.

"Never," I breathed out, and my middle finger was broken next.

How much more of this can I take?

"If anything between us was real, then you'll set me free. Please, Isaac." I pleaded with the Vampire.

Bending another finger back, he grinned. "It wasn't."

Eighteen

lone in the darkness of the cell, I clutched my throbbing hand, the agony of broken fingers pulsating through every nerve. Isaac's chilling words echoed in my mind, a cruel reminder of the dire situation I found myself in.

"Think about your options," he had said, leaving me to grapple with the uncertainty of my fate.

Using the tattered remnants of my torn dress, I fashioned a makeshift sling for my injured hand, a feeble attempt to alleviate the pain that radiated from my shattered fingers. The cold, damp air of the cell seeped into my bones, and I curled up on the wretched cot, attempting to find any consolation in the darkness that enveloped me.

Sleep offered no reprieve from the torment. Nightmares swarmed around me, threatening to engulf my sanity. In the twisted landscapes of my dreams, Isaac loomed as a predatory specter, stalking towards me. Each step he took reverberated with my fears, a haunting refrain that intensified the sense of dread that permeated my subconscious.

The visions of shadows closing in on me left me gasping for breath, a suffocating sensation that mirrored the helplessness of my predicament. As the wraith-like figures converged, their formless shapes danced with the sinister glee of impending doom. I fought against the encroaching darkness, a futile struggle that mirrored the battle I faced in the waking world.

Amidst the nightmarish symphony, another vision tormented my restless mind—a vivid tableau of my aunt Evelyn, her eyes gleaming with a satisfied spark as she seized the grimoire, the key to my family's ancient magic. The shadows that surrounded her seemed to bow in deference, acknowledging her absolute authority over the Realm of Shadow and Bone.

The nightmares blended into a twisted tapestry of fear and despair, each strand weaving a narrative of impending doom. Alone in the cold confines of the cell, I clung to the tattered shreds of my makeshift sling, a fragile anchor in the storm of uncertainty that raged within me. The pain of my broken fingers mingled with the echoes of my nightmares, creating a discord of suffering that seemed to stretch into an eternity of darkness.

———

I jolted awake, my heart pounding in my chest, the pieces of the nightmares clinging to my consciousness like a suffocating fog. The cold reality of the cell enveloped me, and I shivered despite the lingering warmth of the dream-induced sweat that clung to my skin. Assessing my injuries in the dim light, I felt the throbbing ache of my broken fingers, swollen and unresponsive.

The bruises that adorned my body painted a grotesque tapestry of pain, each contusion a testament to the merciless torment I had endured. The knife wound on my chest had ceased bleeding, but the sticky residue left me anxious about the looming threat of infection.

The solitude of the cell persisted, no savior or tormentor emerging from the shadows. The air hung heavy with silence, broken only by the ragged cadence of my breath. I yearned for a reprieve from the relentless darkness that surrounded me, a glimmer of hope that seemed elusive in this desolate abyss.

A bottle of water, tossed callously into the cell while I slept, offered a meager consolation. Its presence hinted at a watchful eye, an unseen observer in the shadows.

As I gingerly picked up the bottle, a pang of thirst urged me to drink, but I wasn't sure when I would see clean water next. Taking a small sip, I used the rest to clean the wound on my chest. I winced in pain. The water eased my worry about infection, but I had nothing to dab the wound with. My dress was too dirty at this point, and I wouldn't even consider the cot.

I cautiously approached the cell bars, the cold iron biting into my fingertips as I peered through the narrow gaps. The dim light in the dungeons offered little assistance in deciphering the shadows that danced beyond my confined space. My eyes strained, seeking any hint of familiarity or a shred of information that could guide me through this labyrinth of uncertainty.

The dungeon's stillness clung to the air, the only audible sound being the hushed breaths that escaped my lips. The stone walls seemed to absorb the feeble glow of the Witchlight, casting an eerie pallor over the cavernous space. As I strained to see beyond the bars, a sense of trepidation settled in the pit of my stomach, amplifying the isolation that permeated the air.

A flicker of movement caught my eye, and I focused my gaze on the shadows that lurked in the corners of the dungeon. The indistinct shapes seemed to mock my attempts to unravel their mysteries. Anxiety gnawed at the edges of my consciousness as I yearned for a glimpse of something recognizable, a tether to the world I knew.

The creature that emerged defied my attempts to categorize it—a grotesque amalgamation of twisted limbs and shadowy features. Its form seemed to defy the laws of nature, a living enigma that made me retch. Fear tightened its grip, and I recoiled, retreating to the safety of my cell.

Isaac's cruel laughter echoed through the damp, cold walls of the dungeon as he entered, a sinister grin etched across his face. I shivered, the chill biting into my already battered body.

"You look terrible," he sneered, relishing in my vulnerability.

His callous comment about my appearance elicited a feeble attempt at defiance, but my weakened state rendered any retort futile. I mustered the strength to lift my gaze, meeting his cold eyes with a mix of defiance and exhaustion. The mockery in his expression sent a jolt of frustration through me, but I clung to what remained of my dignity.

"Are you ready to summon the grimoire?" he inquired, his tone laced with a twisted sense of amusement.

I shook my head, defiance flickering in my eyes.

Isaac's gaze shifted, and he made a subtle gesture. In response, the air grew heavier, and the shadows coalesced into a nightmarish form. A Wraith, an entity of darkness and decay, materialized beside him.

As the Wraith floated towards me, I pressed myself against the cold stone wall, my gaze locked on the grotesque figure. The stench of decay filled the air, and a suffocating dread settled over me. A wicked satisfaction gleamed in his eyes as he watched the Wraith advance.

The Wraith's presence loomed, and I racked my brain for any knowledge I possessed about them. Wraiths were spectral entities, shadows given form and purpose by malevolent intent. They were harbingers of fear and conduits of darkness, capable of inducing

Isaac instructed the Wraith. "Petrify her."

The Wraith hovered closer. Its form twisted and contorted, a grotesque silhouette against the dungeon's dim light. In the blink of an eye, the world around me blurred as an oppressive darkness enveloped my senses.

My vision became a vortex of shadows, and I clutched the cold bars of my cot, a surge of panic seizing my chest. The Wraith had manifested a suffocating aura, penetrating the core of my being. Fear, raw and primal, consumed me, rendering me helpless against the onslaught.

Someone help me. Anyone. Please.

I could hear Isaac stalk towards me with predatory grace. His footsteps echoed ominously, each sound amplifying the dread that gripped my soul. His presence pressed down on me, intensifying the fear that coiled in my veins.

Blind and paralyzed by terror, I awaited whatever cruel fate the Vampire had in store. I was only a pawn, in this game of shadows and cruelty.

Nineteen

"Get away from her!" A familiar voice I'd never thought I'd hear again yelled at the Vampire, and I soon felt a gust of enchanted wind shove Isaac against the wall.

Against all odds, Adrian Grayson had found me.

The clash of bodies echoed through the cell block. Huddled in the corner of my cell, cradling my broken fingers, I watched as Adrian, the one glimmer of hope in this abyss, faced Isaac in a desperate struggle.

Adrian fought with a ferocity born of determination, his movements swift and calculated. But Isaac proved a formidable opponent. My heart pounded in my chest as I witnessed the brutal dance between two opposing forces, each move a step closer to salvation or damnation.

As the skirmish unfolded, a realization dawned

upon me—Adrian didn't know about the black salt lining the cells. Unaware of the nullifying effect, he found his Occult abilities weakened, his strength waning against Isaac's relentless assault.

It was clear to me that Adrian expected this to be a battle of magic, not brute strength. Isaac's demonic laughter sliced through the chaos, a sound that reverberated with the shadows' delight. He seized the advantage, overpowering Adrian with a strength that defied mortal limits.

With a forceful slam, Isaac hurled Adrian back. The impact resonated through the cell block, a testament to the Occult's powerlessness in the face of Isaac's ruthless authority. Adrian, disoriented but defiant, staggered to his feet. Isaac, quick to exploit the situation, moved with predatory grace to seal the cell door.

The heavy clang of metal echoed, sealing both Adrian and me within our respective cages. The cell, once a harbinger of isolation, now became a shared prison of shadows. The Wraith disappeared with a wail, and Isaac hissed.

The Vampire's coal-black eyes bore into ours, a glint of cruel satisfaction in his gaze. "Evelyn won't be pleased with this interference," he hissed, the words hanging in the air like a grim prophecy. "You've only delayed the inevitable, and punishment will be swift."

Isaac's parting words crouched in the shadows, a promise of retribution that sent a chill down my spine.

———

We were silent as we listened to Isaac's angry footsteps down the hall. Adrian's eyes looked haunted, and met mine as he spoke, the weight of his words hanging in the air like a pall of remorse. "I'm sorry, Iris. I tried to get to you in time, but I failed."

His voice, heavy with self-blame, intertwined with the shadows that always clung to the walls. The confines of our shared prison seemed to tighten, the air thick with the unspoken weight of our shared fate.

"I noticed you leave the ball after you spoke to that Witch," Adrian continued, his gaze distant as he recounted the events. "When you didn't return, I knew something was wrong. That's when I saw Isaac dragging you away."

The memory of Isaac's grip tightened around my throat, the visceral recollection of the force that had torn me from the revelry. "I ran to get Thalia and Ewan," he explained, a hint of frustration coloring his words. "But I could only find Thalia. With her Werecat senses, we found the mausoleum where Isaac had taken you. It took us days to figure out how to open the crypt, and I only just found you."

Adrian's admission hung in the silence, a confession of the imperfect timing that had marked our desperate attempt at escape. The regret etched across his face mirrored the guilt that nestled within my own chest.

I searched his eyes, a question heavy on my lips. "Where's Thalia?"

Adrian's gaze faltered, a flicker of vulnerability betraying the turmoil within him. "I asked her to go get help," he admitted. "I couldn't leave you alone. When I got to your cell I intended to come up with an effective plan of escape. But I couldn't bear to watch Isaac hurt you. I attacked him without much of a plan."

I gingerly took Adrian's chin in my non-injured hand, his gaze meeting mine with remorse. The shadows danced in the dim light of the cell, casting a veil over our shared vulnerability. With a quiet but emotional gratitude, I thanked him for his courage, my voice barely above a whisper.

"Thank you, Adrian," I murmured, the words carrying the immensity of our shared ordeal. "For risking so much to save me."

His russet eyes, a storm of conflicting emotions, bore into mine. In the hushed stillness of the cell, our worlds collided in a tumult of fear and unspoken connection. The tension between us was palpable, a thread that seemed to weave fate into the very fabric of our existence.

Without words, our lips met in a passionate kiss. In that stolen moment, the shadows receded, leaving only the warmth of our entwined spirits.

As we pulled apart, a lingering curiosity tugged at my heart.

"Adrian," I said, the question hanging in the air, "*why* were you willing to charge into danger for me? We hardly know each other."

His gaze softened. "From the moment I met you, Iris," he confessed, "I couldn't get you out of my head. And I'd ever be able to live with myself if there was something I could do to help, and I just sat idly by."

He really is my knight in shining armor.

Our fingers intertwined. "Iris," Adrian spoke, his voice a gentle affirmation of the uncharted path we now walked together, "we'll find a way out of this. We won't let the shadows consume us."

We kissed again, slowly at first and then more fervently. I pulled at the collar on his shirt, and he pulled me tightly to him. I pushed my fingers through his dark hair, and hissed in pain when I remembered my broken fingers.

"I didn't mean to take advantage of you in your pain," Adrian extracted his mouth from mine and quickly apologized.

I blushed. The adrenaline from his rescue attempt, mixed with the fear of confinement must be the reason behind the unexpected kiss.

Maybe he's not the arrogant playboy I had thought him to be. I hope we live long enough so I can find out.

He began to speak, and his words wove a tale of familial bonds and aspirations that defied my preconceived notions.

"My mom is an HearthWitch, skilled in weaving magic into our home. She raised me and my two older brothers with love and enchantment," Adrian shared, his voice carrying a hint of nostalgia. "My father, on the other hand, built his tech empire from the ground up. He's also the leader of the NorthEast Equinox Coven."

"All I've ever wanted was to follow in my father's footsteps," he confessed, his gaze distant as if envisioning the path he sought to tread. "But I haven't found my specialty yet, and I can feel my dad's disappointment."

"What about your brothers? What paths have they chosen?"

Adrian's eyes regained focus, and he willingly delved into the tales of his siblings. "One of my brothers is continuing his warlock education with a group of magical high priests in the north. He's dedicated to unraveling the ancient mysteries of our craft.

The other is pursuing a medical degree and training with a magical healer to become a healer for our Coven."

"I was raised by Thalia's family after my parents' deaths," I said, the echoes of my words reverberating in the confined space. "My parents, fated mates, were powerful Sorcerers. I'm sure you're aware of the theory that children born from such unions would inherit a potent magical lineage."

I paused, the weight of my parents' loss overshadowing my narrative. "But it's more of a myth, I think. I don't feel more powerful than usual, and without my family's grimoire until recently, my magical skills had stagnated. I'm afraid I won't be much help getting us out of here."

"And then there's my aunt Evelyn," I continued, tracing the contours of my painful history. "She's the Queen of Shadows, the orchestrator of all this chaos. Her motives are shrouded in darkness. She wants the grimoire. And she wants all mortals dead." I shivered.

"Iris, you're not your aunt," Adrian reassured me, his voice a soothing balm in the midst of our shared turmoil. "And this isn't your fault." His sincerity resonated in the confined space, creating a fragile sanctuary against the encroaching darkness.

We settled on the cold cot, wrapped in each other's arms, as if the warmth we generated could ward off the chill of the Shadow Realm. The quietude of the cell was disrupted only by the rhythmic cadence of our breaths, a shared lullaby that carried us into the realm of dreams.

In the serenity of our entwined slumber, the shadows seemed to retreat, allowing a fragile respite from the perils that awaited us. As we surrendered to the embrace of sleep, I clung to the belief that our intertwined fates held the promise of a dawn beyond the looming darkness.

TWENTY

"Wake up, lovebirds," Isaac sneered, his presence a dark cloud that hung over us. "Torturing you will be so much more entertaining now that you can watch each other."

The hopeful warmth that had cocooned us the night before turned cold, replaced by the ominous chill of impending torment. Adrian and I, entangled in each other's arms, were now confronted by the harsh reality of our predicament.

Isaac's voice cut through the stagnant air of our cell. "Evelyn is ready to see you," he sneered, the ominous tone underscoring the gravity of the impending encounter. "I hope you're ready, Iris," Isaac continued, a twisted anticipation in his gaze. "Evelyn is not in the mood for games. She wants that grimoire, and she wants it now."

Evelyn's wrath loomed like a shadowed specter, and the menacing energy seemed to seep through the very walls that held us captive. Isaac, reveling in our vulnerability, threw two pairs of black salt cuffs into the room with a grin. The metallic clatter echoed, a harsh punctuation to the foreboding atmosphere that surrounded us.

"Put them on," he commanded, his voice a cold edict that brooked no defiance.

With reluctant compliance, we each took a pair, the gritty texture of the black salt biting into our skin as we fastened them around our wrists. The metallic click of the cuffs closing felt like a solemn echo, sealing our shared fate in the face of impending judgment.

Isaac led the way through the labyrinthine corridors, each step echoing with the burden of impending doom. The shadows danced around us, conspiring to suffocate any remnants of hope that clung desperately to our hearts. "The shadows like you," the Vampire noted.

"The shadows? What do you mean?" I asked him.

"You stupid bitch. Do you think Queen Evelyn calls it the 'Court of Shadows' for nothing?" The Vampire rolled his eyes, and squeezed my broken fingers playfully.

I winced, and Adrian looked murderously at the

sadistic Occult. "Fuck you, Isaac. Don't you *ever* fucking touch her," he spat out.

Isaac grinned. "I'll do as I please, pretty boy."

————

As we approached the throne room, a chilling aura emanated from within. Evelyn awaited us on her onyx throne, and tapped her purple nails impatiently. "Iris," Evelyn's voice cut through the silence. "You continue to defy me. The grimoire must be summoned, and you *will* be the one to do it."

I noted the throne room was adorned with her Court of Shadows. Writhing like restless spirits, they bore witness to our impending judgment. Evelyn's eyes, pools of darkness that seemed to pierce through our very souls, fixed on me with a wrathful intensity.

"I won't do it," I replied, my voice a trembling but defiant whisper. "I won't help you rid the world of mortals."

Her eyebrows raised. "Rid the world? If I did that, then who would be our slaves?" A cruel smile materialized in place of her surprise. "But, very well, Iris. If you won't comply, perhaps seeing someone else pay your price will motivate you."

Isaac seized Adrian, his grip unyielding, and dragged him before the Shadow Queen. Evelyn's gaze shifted from me to him, a predatory glint surfacing in her eyes.

"Adrian," she purred, the word dripping with menace. "Iris's disobedience will be your burden to bear."

My heart pounded with fear as Evelyn's decree endured like a death knell. I pleaded with the queen to focus her wrath on me, to spare Adrian from the torment that awaited. "Punish me instead," I implored, the desperation in my voice revealing the depths of my fear. "Leave him out of this."

But Evelyn, her heart cloaked in shadows, dismissed my plea with a wave of her hand. "No, Iris. He will learn the consequences of your defiance."

Adrian, his face a mask of stoic resolve, met my gaze with a whispered reassurance. "Don't give in, Iris. I can handle whatever she throws at me."

He doesn't deserve this. I don't think he realizes just how ruthless my aunt can be.

"Oh?" the queen smirked. She snapped her fingers and the Dark Elf that was once my escort materialized out of the shadows and bowed.

"Give that pretty face of his some character," Evelyn commanded, her voice cutting through the silence like a blade. "Let the echoes of his pain resonate through these halls."

Evelyn's decree echoed through the throne room, a

chilling proclamation that shattered the fragile sanctuary of my hope. The ominous air thickened as her third-in-command seized Adrian with an iron grip. The impending torment cast a suffocating pall over us, leaving me paralyzed with fear.

Adrian's protests, a symphony of anguished yells, reached my ears—a chilling prelude to the torment that awaited him in the unseen corners of the castle. The shadows writhed in delight, feeding on the fear that permeated the air.

"Stop! Please, stop!" I pleaded, the words escaping my lips in desperate supplication. "He's done nothing wrong. Punish me instead."

Evelyn, an inscrutable silhouette on her ominous throne, remained unmoved by my pleas. Her eyes bore into mine with a cold detachment that sent shivers down my spine.

"He will suffer until you comply, Iris," she declared, the shadows echoing her cruel resolve. "Summon the grimoire, and it will all end."

The ominous ultimatum hung in the air like a curse. My heart raced with the heft of an unbearable decision—sacrifice my own defiance to save Adrian from the clutches of the shadows or endure his torment, clinging to the last shreds of our shared resistance.

I can't let her win.

"No," I whispered, the word a tremulous declaration of my refusal. "I won't let you use him against me. This is bigger than the two of us."

Evelyn's gaze, unyielding and shadowed, betrayed no hint of mercy. "Begin," she said to the Dark Elf.

The silent dungeon air was shattered by the sudden, guttural sound of a blade slicing through the space. I jolted awake, disoriented, as the echoes of the grim act reverberated through the cold walls. My eyes widened in horror as I took in the scene unfolding before me.

Adrian writhed in pain, his hands clutching his face. A deep gash marred his once-smooth features, the cruel handiwork of Evelyn's command. The sight of blood staining his pale skin made me cry out.

The Dark Elf lingered in the shadows, his blade still gleaming with the residue of Adrian's blood. The aftermath of the brutal act was a grotesque tableau of pain and submission. In the eerie stillness that followed, I could only clench my fists in silent fury.

Evelyn's reign of terror will not go unanswered.

"Do you still doubt my words, Iris?" Evelyn asked, her voice a sinister cadence that cut through the ominous silence. "Let me dispel your skepticism."

A gesture from the shadow queen, and Isaac stalked towards us. My heart pounded with apprehension in the looming darkness. The shadows converged, casting their judgment upon the throne room.

"Yes, mistress?" Isaac breathed to the Shadow Queen. I looked at Adrian, laying on the marble floor, clutching his face.

"Break his spirit," the queen ordered.

I recoiled, horror etched across my face, as the entire weight of Isaac's foot descended upon Adrian's fragile form. The gut-wrenching sound of breaking ribs echoed through the cold dungeon. Adrian's body convulsed in agony.

My hands instinctively reached towards him, a futile attempt to reach out and shield him from the merciless onslaught. The helplessness gnawed at my insides. Isaac stood over Adrian's limp figure with a sinister satisfaction. His eyes, devoid of empathy, reveled in the grotesque display of dominance.

She's going to kill him. I can't bear much more of this, and he can't either.

"Is this enough proof of my motivation, Iris?" Evelyn sneered, her satisfaction palpable. "Your precious *savior* is at my mercy."

My breath caught in my throat as Adrian lay crumbled on the cool stone. "Adrian," I murmured, the name a fragile plea that sought to bridge the chasm of despair. "Are you... alive?"

he nodded weakly. "I'm here, Iris. Don't give in."

Adrian," I whispered helplessly, my voice a fragile thread in the tapestry of the shadows' judgment.

Evelyn's eyes, dark and unyielding, flickered with annoyance as Adrian remained defiant in the face of his torment. "Isaac," Evelyn commanded, "Show the little warlock the futility of resistance."

Isaac advanced with a venomous glint in his eyes. The ominous silence that followed was broken only by the echo of Adrian's moans of pain. He shook his head —a silent vow to endure, even in the face of the impending torment.

Adrian, an inch away from the abyss of death, clung to the threads of his fading strength. "The stars above might seem distant and cold, but they're burning with an enduring fire," he wheezed out. "Our light persists even when it feels like the world is shrouded in shadows."

The shadows closed in as Isaac's cruelty reached its zenith.

———

"I'll do it," I choked out, my voice a trembling surrender to the shadows that encroached on my soul. "I'll summon the grimoire. Just—spare him."

Evelyn's triumphant smile cut through the shadows like a cruel dagger. She lifted a manicured hand, and Isaac paused his cruel assault on the man willing to forfeit his life for me.

"Iris," Adrian gasped, the words a raspy breath that clung to life. "Don't—"

But I ignored him, the summoning spell already in motion. I chanted the last words, and slowly the leather-bound grimoire materialized in my hands. The tome's weight in my hands was a reminder of the choices I had made—a dark pact to spare the lives of those I loved. Evelyn reached for the ancient book, her eyes gleaming with insanity.

"Finally," she sneered, her voice echoing through the throne room.

The shadows quivered with anticipation as she raced down the steps of her throne and grasped the grimoire.

"Isaac," Evelyn commanded, her voice a venomous decree. "Take the Warlock's life as punishment for my niece's defiance."

TWENTY-ONE

Isaac quickly raised his hand to deliver the final blow. The shadows gathered, closing in on my condemned friend. In that moment of impending tragedy, fear and desperation surged within me. With an unintentional scream, a primal release of anguish, I reached into the depths of my power.

"Adrian!"

Waves of Hellfire erupted, an inferno that defied the shadows' control. I stood amidst the chaos, my eyes wide with astonishment at the torrent of power I had unwittingly unleashed.

Evelyn's triumphant sneer twisted into a mask of terror as the flames consumed the throne room. The shadows recoiled in the face of the uncontrollable blaze. Isaac, too, stumbled back, his composure shattered by the unexpected eruption of my magic. Panic etched across Evelyn's face as the inferno raged, its fury uncontainable.

"How the hell–" the Shadow Queen was forced back a step, and her grip on the grimoire loosened. Taking my only advantage, I snatched the book out of her hands and situated myself squarely in the Hellfire. The once-imposing throne room started to crumble, shattered by the unexpected surge of the otherworldly flames.

"Retreat!" Evelyn commanded, her voice a desperate admission of defeat. The Shadow Court, once poised for cruelty, scattered in the face of the untamed Hellfire.

As the shadows retreated, Evelyn's parting words cut through the crackling flames. "I *will* find you, Iris. And when I do, there will be no sanctuary for you to hide. Your destiny is entwined with shadows, and they *will* consume you."

The ominous echoes of Evelyn's promise lingered, a forewarning of the shadows' inevitable return, as the flames whispered of the infernal wrath that had briefly shattered their control. The acrid scent of smoke lingered in the air as the remaining shadows flew out of the throne room, the Hellfire still roaring in the distance. The shadows had dispersed, their ominous presence retreating before the unbridled inferno. My heart raced, a mixture of relief and urgency propelling me forward.

My focus shifted to Adrian, who lay weakened on the cold stone floor. "We need to get out of here," he mumbled.

I managed to lift him, and carefully but quickly navigated the corridors of the palace; the once ominous atmosphere now replaced by the disarray of a Shadow Court in retreat. The crypt portal loomed ahead. No blood offering was required this time, we were already covered in it.

———

Once inside the mausoleum, I laid Adrian gently on the cold stone floor, the echoes of his pain etched on his battered face. The shadows of the otherworldly palace were replaced by the cool, silent embrace of the tomb.

As Adrian struggled to maintain consciousness, he implored me to lend him some of my power to send a magical beacon to his Coven. His strength waning, he collapsed against the crypt's cold stone surface. The air around us crackled with magic as I held him close to me.

Please work. Please work.

The mausoleum's silence pressed upon us as we

awaited the response to Adrian's arcane flare. He lay before me, his life flickering like a frail candle. I attempted to channel healing spells with a determination born of desperation—an effort to mend wounds beyond my skill. My hands trembled, whispers of arcane energy dancing around my fingertips. But the healing magic eluded me. Only minor bruises yielded to my efforts, leaving the gravest wounds untouched.

"Come on," I muttered, frustration etched across my face. "I can do this."

I watched as Adrian's life force dwindled, each passing moment echoing with the dread of impending loss.

Please hang on a little longer.

The mausoleum's silence pressed upon us as we awaited the response to Adrian's flare. He lay before me, his life flickering like a frail candle in the darkness. Adrian's shallow breaths sounded like a haunting lament, a melody of life slipping away. My efforts persisted, my desperation manifesting in each futile attempt to coax vitality back into his failing form.

Just as hope seemed to wane, a sudden burst of energy surged through the mausoleum. An unfamiliar man materialized alongside me, and I flinched.

"Who the hell are you?" I screeched at him, and covered Adrian with my body.

"I'm the Equinox healer you summoned. Now

move back and let me work," the man spoke brusquely.

The man assessed Adrian's condition, his brow furrowing with the heaviness of a somber diagnosis. Even I could see that Adrian clung to the fragile thread that connected him to the realm of the living.

"He's in good hands," the healer spoke, his voice a soothing balm to my frayed nerves. "I'm the best at what I do."

I clung to his words and buried my head in my hands. "We need a miracle," I whispered.

The healer worked diligently, his hands weaving intricate patterns of magic over Adrian's prone form. As seconds stretched into minutes, a subtle change brushed over Adrian's ashen features. A faint glow, a promise of renewal, emanated from the healer's hands.

"He's stabilizing," the healer announced, his words a melody of relief that resonated in the chamber. "But he's not out of the woods yet."

In the gentle glow of the healer's magic, Adrian's breaths steadied—a fragile yet resilient rhythm that echoed the promise of a new beginning.

Adrian's parents arrived, and gasped when they saw their youngest son in critical condition. Adrian's father reached down to take his son into his arms, and his mother wiped a few errant tears. "We need to get him to the healer's den."

Like a wild animal, I moved on my own accord, and clutched Adrian's hand. After everything he had done for me, I couldn't bear to be parted from him, not knowing how he fared with the healers.

"We'll update you once he's settled," Adrian's father added, the lines of concern etched on his face. "And we expect an explanation for all of this once we've all rested."

Reluctantly, I let go of Adrian's hand and nodded tiredly at the Coven leader. "I promise I'll explain everything."

They took the steps two at a time, leaving me in the mausoleum with the healer. Swiftly and with practiced ease, the healing magic worked its wonders. My relieved sigh was mirrored in the healer's eyes as the pain in my fingers subsided.

He paused when he reached the ugly, half-healed wound on my chest. "I'm afraid I can't remove this scar," the healer confessed, his expression sympathetic. "The weapon used to create your laceration was imbued with rock salt; intended to make a lasting impression." The healer grimaced.

"That's okay," I replied, meeting his gaze with a steely resolve. "It will serve as a reminder—a reminder of the cruelty the Shadow Queen is capable of, and the strength needed to defy her."

The healer looked at me in terror when I

mentioned the queen. "You– you met with the Shadow Queen... and lived to tell the tale?" He choked out.

I nodded and ran my fingers lightly over my scar. "Evelyn will return," I stated, my voice resolute. "With a vengeance."

COMING SOON...

Tranquility is but a fragile illusion as the ominous presence of the Shadow Queen continues to haunt the mortal realm, casting a dark cloud over the lives of Occults. As fear spreads like wildfire, Iris learns that to confront the looming threat, she must unravel the mysteries hidden within her own family tree.

Amid the impending danger, Adrian and Iris must navigate the delicate balance between their budding romance and the looming darkness that threatens to consume everything they hold dear. Will their connection be the key to unlocking Iris's true potential, or will the Shadow Queen's malevolent forces shatter the stability they so desperately seek?

SECRETS
OF SILVER GROVE
BOOK TWO

LEGACY

BLY
FORSYTHE

Afterword

Thank you for buying my book! I really hope you enjoyed it. The continued support, by purchasing my books, helps support me so I can continue writing for my readers. Feel free to loan this out to other readers, I just ask that they *please* buy a copy if they like it. This helps tell my publisher how many people are reading my book, and of course - it helps me write more books.

Thanks again! If I'm ever in your area signing books, please stop by and say hello! I'd love to meet you.

Enjoy the book, and don't forget to leave a review!

Made in the USA
Columbia, SC
03 June 2024

36170225R00121